UNBEATEN

Dawn of Deception, Book 3

A. R. SHAW

Apocalyptic Ventures, LLC

Copyright © 2019 by A. R. Shaw

All rights reserved.

No part of this book may be reproduced in any form or by any electronic or mechanical means, including information storage and retrieval systems, without written permission from the author, except for the use of brief quotations in a book review.

For those of you, unbeaten.

In the midst of chaos, there is also opportunity.

— SUN TZU

INTRODUCTION

Astoria, Oregon

"You are my sunshine..."

"Baby, look at Mommy." She gently laid her hand on the side of her son's face and pulled it into her side. Her younger boy already held his eyes tightly shut. Desperately, she tried to shield them from what was about to unfold.

The warehouse, devoid of any equipment, was crowded with people pushing and shoving, their voices echoing in the void above them. The cold didn't mask the putrid air of so many bodies in one place. They should be used to the funk smell of man by now but that wouldn't matter much longer, she reminded herself.

"...my only sunshine."

On a stage in the front, Tale spoke. She'd heard the speech many times before. But he repeated it nonetheless. "The rules are simple. Only I make the rules. Anyone in violation of the rules will no longer exist. The rules are as follows: 1) No dependents without representation. 2) Three generations of punishment for

INTRODUCTION

crimes committed. 3) Do what you're told in the time allowed. 4) Meetings are mandatory. 5) No one discusses my business."

"...you make me happy, when skies are gray."

Olivia felt the humming from her son's throat against her thigh. Her younger son pulled his finger from his mouth and buried his head into her leg as well, picking up the familiar tune. It was something she'd unconsciously taught them to do when violence erupted around them. She also began to sing the song under her breath, patting their heads and swaying as they clung to her.

"...you'll never know, dear, how much I love you..."

"These people behind me are in violation of one or more of the rules," Tale continued.

The back of his dark, bald head was all she saw. She could not help her fleeting glances to the right and the left exits, where the armed guards stood. There was no way out. She knew that without looking. Her friend and her two boys were doing the same thing, but a sense of peace and resignation came over her. Quietly the other mother sobbed and clenched her hands tight with her arms around her crying sons. They stood together with several other doomed residents of Astoria they'd somehow met along the way. She'd never been on the stage before, always the observer of the madness from the other side.

"...please don't take...my sunshine away."

I

DAVIS

A gate hung in the distance. Not just any gate. This wasn't a wire fencing contraption. It would be absurd to think one could slide this thing away on little rusty rollers to the side at some warehouse compound. It wasn't a prison gate topped with wire razor, either. No one would describe this gateway as flimsy. It wasn't even something you'd find at a military base, Fort Knox, or a royal palace. No...this damn thing was summoned out of the dark medieval past and brought to the present era for an exact purpose. Strength, intimidation, we kick ass here: that's what it said. By the looks of it, the gray metal overlapped with spiked riveting protruding in nearly aligned intervals. Rust highlighted the crevices. At over sixteen feet tall, the gateway to the oceanside town of Cannon Beach, Oregon, connected to an equally intimidating barrier along either side.

No one was visible along the top, no one aiming at them as their vehicles rumbled to a stop before it. The weirdest thing of all, the gate just stood there. As massive as it was, they saw within the city walls because the damn thing was left open a few feet.

"What the hell is that?"

Davis clenched his jaw slowly as he chewed the stale gum in his mouth, not wasting time answering the driver's question.

The engines idled a little louder than they should. Davis remained in thought. Tale wasn't going to like this. Their purpose was to get in there and teach these poor fools a lesson. He now had the sneaking suspicion they were the lesson learners today, though that thought slipped his mind quickly.

Davis's eyes remained on the unexpected entryway as he said, "Tell Marvin that ethanol's running a little high. Engine's going to throw a rod."

"WIL-CO," Jerry said with a little stutter. Jerry was always a little nervous. That was his *normal* mode. That's why Davis turned a blind eye anytime he snorted something up his nose, drank too much, or otherwise took anything to calm the hell down.

Lifting his arm up and out the window, he gave the signal and the other two vehicles behind them cut their engines. Davis sat in place a while longer, taking in the sounds. The ocean waves came in off to the right. They couldn't see the beach over the dunes. The wind blew through their opened windows. Jerry began to open the truck door, causing a clinking. "Wait," David said. "Just wait a minute."

"Why would they build something that well and leave it open like that?" Jerry said.

Another rhetorical question.

"Maybe they left and didn't bother shutting it? They had to know we were coming for them. Why didn't they just leave? The smart ones vanish."

Jerry let out a huff. "None of this was here the last time we came to pick up a load. They took down Hyde, destroyed the complex, and now this? Who are these people?"

Davis listened as Jerry thought out loud. It's what they did. Jerry basically talked to himself as Davis listened. Sometimes...only sometimes, there was a bit of logic that had eluded

Davis' thoughts in the past, and those little nuggets were worth gleaning from his young junkie friend.

"Only one way to find out what's going on," Davis said as he exited the truck. Slamming his door caused a nearby bird to dart from a wave-torn rhododendron bush.

The small caravan consisted of three vehicles. Jerry motioned for the others to get ready. Ten other men joined them. They walked slowly, transfixed by the monstrosity before them.

One of the men, their engineer, came up and eagerly said, "What do you make of that thing?" Marvin pointed with his eyes wide. "Hasn't been up very long. It's only just begun to rust. Made of scraps. Some good welders put that together quick."

"That's not the point. Why's it open?" Davis said. "That's what I want to know."

Marvin shook his head. "I don't know. It's meant to keep people out. If it were locked, we'd have a hell of a time getting through there. Look at the locking mechanism."

"That's what I mean. It's not really a gate then, is it?"

"Maybe the darn kids ran off and left it open," Jerry said.

"No...it's a message," Davis said. After spitting out his stale gum he motioned for them to follow.

It was time.

"Let's get in there and give them a message of our own."

2

SLOANE

T*wo weeks before.*

THEY ALL LOOKED AT HER EXPECTANTLY. THE WIND BLEW OFF the beach, careening little sharp grains of stinging sand into the side of her face. The sun sat just beyond Haystack Rock, though the flame torches surrounding them kept them in the glowing light of dusk.

"We've worked very hard to prepare for this. I'm thankful we've finally come to share a meal together. It's long overdue. Everyone brought a little something from your personal stores and that means a lot now in this time of scarcity. It means we've bonded. We trust one another. And now we have the opportunity to get to know ourselves as a group a little more."

By the flame, she looked at their faces as they sat around the picnic tables before her. Everyone bundled in extra layers to keep warm from the evening's harsh coastal wind. A few of them always held back on the periphery. She noted Boyd's face back there, his sad eyes reflecting the fire flames. She once hated him but now she only held pity for the young man. His sister was lost to them for now. Nicole, too. She was unreachable most of the time, refusing to speak. Only Mae could keep her engaged, though in silence.

Mae held Nicole close to her for warmth, constantly making sure she knew she was loved and needed, never letting her out of her sight. It was an endless effort. Then there were Chuck, Kent, and the old man, they and several others constantly scanning the outer realm, a habit they wouldn't soon forget.

In her soul, Sloane knew this was possibly the calm before the storm. They would come soon. Some of these faces would fade in battle. Some of them would triumph and some would fail altogether. That time was coming. She could feel it. And they weren't ready. There were lessons yet to learn and little time to teach them.

"I'm going to tell you a story," Sloane said as she stood before them.

Chuck lifted a spoon to his mouth. He looked as if he wanted to say something then, as she stared into his eyes, he thought better of it.

As she cut her attention to Wren, leaning against a pole at the side, her daughter rolled her eyes at the mention of a story. And then just behind her daughter to the right was Jason, his protective gaze always upon her daughter, though Wren didn't know it yet.

They were all so precious. Each life. So many souls here. So much to lose.

"Yes, a story." She cleared her throat. "I'm paraphrasing, of course, but in Sun Tzu's theory of managing soldiers in *The Art of War*, King Ho Lu challenged him to display his military prowess. Sun Tzu agreed. Then the king asked him if he could apply the test to women. Sun Tzu agreed. Then the king asked if the test could apply to his 180 concubines. Again, Sun Tzu agreed.

"He split the group of women in half and then selected the two most prized concubines as officers of each group. He then gave them all spears and taught them simple directions such as: front and back, left hand and right, eyes front, left turn, right turn, and about turn. Simple enough, right?" she said nodding her head with a smile.

Many of them agreed with full mouths, their eyes upon her still. The story was a lesson and it was working.

"Then Sun Tzu gave the order along with the sound of battle drums. 'Right turn.'

"Nothing but laughter came from the girls. I can imagine them, with their feminine mirth, nearly knocking one another over with the wooden spears they carried. This wasn't their world. They were concubines, meant for beauty. They were not soldiers meant for battle. But at this moment they were cast as soldiers and they were given the rules, and this was a test. They just didn't know the game they were playing. That part was never revealed to them...in the beginning.

"Sun Tzu said, 'If words of commands are not clear and distinct and orders are not thoroughly understood, then it's the general's fault.' So he went through the process again. He explained the rules of the game and gave a new command at the end. This time he said, 'Left turn'. Again, the girls bumped into one another and began laughing.

"Sun Tzu said, 'If words of commands are not clear and distinct and orders are not understood, the general is to blame. But...if orders are clear and the soldiers disobey, then it is the fault of the officers.'

"Because of their failures he ordered the beheading of both concubine officers. The king objected and tried to intervene, saying that Sun Tzu's military prowess had passed the test. They were his most prized concubines, after all. But Sun Tzu said there were certain orders of His Majesty's that he was unable to accept.

And he had the concubine officers beheaded and then selected two more."

"God, Mom," Mae said. "Harsh."

Sloane smiled but ignored her younger daughter as she continued. "This time, when given the orders the girls followed through without flaw. Then Sun Tzu sent a message to the king saying that his soldiers were properly drilled and disciplined. 'Bid them go through fire and water, and they will not disobey.'"

She ended the story and picked up her own neglected bowl of stew.

"So you're saying we should follow orders or you'll behead us?" Chuck asked.

"No. I'm saying if you don't follow orders there's a price to pay. We are not a well-trained army. I'm not a great general. I don't expect us to win every battle, but I expect us to communicate and adjust as needed. I expect us to be prepared for what's coming. I expect us to defend and protect what we have here. I expect us to fight back."

Chuck swallowed another spoonful and nodded his head.

"If we don't fight back," she continued, "there are dire consequences."

"It won't be easy," he said, waving his spoon in the air between bites, making eye contact with her.

"Nothing worth having is ever easy. Funny how freedom is like that...an ever-living battle...even in the apocalypse."

3
DAVIS

A tingle ran up his spine as he slid the barrel of his rifle along the edge of the gate's rough metal. Through his sights he saw no certain enemy yet as the gate inched forward. In a athletic stance, with his shoulders squared up with the potential target, he stood aiming, ready, and when the gate finally budged opened enough for him to have a clear view of the interior, he stood astonished. The others in his command entered as well and when they had a clear view of the enemy's realm, only an old man stood before them.

What was odder...the old man ignored their invasion as he continued his work of sweeping the street with his back turned to them.

Only three blocks in distance away, unless the old man was totally deaf with his back to them, he had to know they were there. "Put your hands up," Davis yelled, though he didn't appear armed sans the push broom.

The old man seemed to not know of their presence.

"I said, put your hands up and drop the broom," Davis yelled again.

Nothing. Three more pushes of the broom. A plume of dust

formed with his efforts. The old man seemed annoyed by a flattened white paper cup on the ground.

"Just shoot him," Jerry said. "Get it over with."

"Nah," he's not armed.

"I'll shoot him, then," Jerry said.

"No. He's just an old man."

Davis aimed at him anyway. He sent off one round. The paper cup went flying like a saucer.

The old man's face darted toward them.

"Put your hands up, now." Davis and the others ran toward him. "Don't move."

The old man stood, trembling, with his arms in the air. By the time they reached him, Davis noticed a dark spot on the old man's khakis.

"He's pissing himself," Jerry said. "That's disgusting. Crappy old bastard."

"Stop it. Keep your eyes open. This could be a trap." Trying to keep his men on alert was always a problem. "Do not get distracted here."

"It's just me," the old man pleaded. "What do you want?"

"I don't think for a minute you made that damn gate all by yourself. You're not fooling me. Where are they?"

"Who?"

Davis looked around. The wide, swept streets. The buildings. Some were in disarray...others neat as a surgical tray. There were trails between debris to some. Others were blockaded. "The people that live here. The ones that took down the compound and killed Hyde. We're not here for a visit. We're here for a reason."

"There's a few of us but they're out scouting for supplies," the old man said and began to lower his arms.

"Don't even."

"I'm not armed."

In a growl, Davis flipped his rifle over and punched the old man in the stomach and yelled, "I said keep your hands in the air."

"This is making me nervous," Jerry said.

"Where are they?" Davis yelled at the old man again.

"They're out," the old man said, doubled over. "You came at a bad time. Try again later."

Davis knew if they were watching him, now would be the time they'd take potshots at them. If he hurt the old man, that would draw them out for an attack. The problem was, he had a hard time hurting the defenseless.

His men were getting jumpy.

"Let's look around. Marvin, check out that old market. Take anything useful. Jerry, that building there. It's too clean, the coffee shop. Check that out."

As he watched his men move off in the distance, the others stood there on guard, watching for anything that moved. Davis kept his rifle pointed on the old man. One false move, a shot at one of his officers, and the old man would die. In the meantime, the smell of urine permeated the immediate surroundings as he listened for any clues from his men.

"Clear," Jerry yelled from the coffee shop.

"Find anything?" Davis asked.

"Nah, smells like coffee but there's nothing in there."

Davis looked to the market. "Marvin?" he yelled.

A second too long passed without a sound.

"Marvin?"

Nothing. Not a peep.

"What the heck? I saw him walk in. Didn't he just go in there?"

Davis grabbed the old man by the shirt and jerked him to his face. "What's going on?"

"I don't know. Nothing!"

"Hey," Marvin called out suddenly, as he appeared in the doorway of the old market. He stuffed something oblong and yellow into his mouth and tried to speak. Waving with his arm, he held up a familiar white box with blue writing and said, "'eck it out. They 'ot 'winkies in 'ere. 'ons of 'em."

That's when Marvin suddenly dropped into nothingness. He stood there one second and then the next, it was like the ground opened up and swallowed him and his Twinkies. A loud clang echoed as he disappeared from sight.

Gripping up on the rifle, Davis couldn't believe his eyes. One second, Marvin was there and the next he'd vanished.

"What just happened?" Jerry yelled.

In quick order, the men scurried to form a defensive outward circle. Davis held the old man at gunpoint in front of them by his shirt. "Keep your eyes open on all sides," Davis said calmly. As a group, they edged back toward the direction they'd come in. They'd gone no more than five feet when the giant metal gate slammed shut with a loud, defining clang.

"Oh...crap! Shoot the old man, Davis," Jerry said.

"Negative. He's the only thing keeping us alive right now."

"They killed Marvin!" Jerry said, and Davis could tell by the tone of his friend's voice that he was about to lose it.

"Calm down, Jerry. As far as we know, Marvin's still eating Twinkies somewhere below ground. We don't know he's dead. He's just missing."

"He dropped down. It was a trap," said one of the other men.

"Probably onto spikes or something. Should we split up?" Jerry asked.

"No, unless you want to end up like Marvin," Davis said calmly. He'd always had the unnerving and unique ability to become calmer in a crisis. "That's what they want. Divide and conquer."

That's when he shook the old man. "Start talking. What the hell is going on here? This some kind of trick?"

Then they all ducked as something exploded. From over the locked mammoth gate, smoke and flames rose from where their vehicles were. Two more explosions followed, one for each vehicle.

The old man started to make a noise.

The muffled crying started low and then morphed into all-out laughter. The old man was laughing his ass off.

The laughter became louder...more jovial. Davis found it unnerving. He didn't want to hold onto him anymore. He shoved him away as if he had leprosy or something equally repulsive, but held his aim.

"Make him stop that," Jerry said.

"Keep it together, everyone," Davis yelled.

But not even Davis could stand the laughter. He backed away another five feet. Heads swiveled everywhere.

That's when tunes began to play on hidden loudspeakers in all directions. Jimi Hendrix's voice bellowed *All Along the Watchtower*. So deafening was the sound, vibrations rattled the soles of their shoes.

Stunned, Davis stood there, unsure what would happen next. His heart pounded five times the beat.

Jerry suddenly stepped forward. Stood erect. Raised his weapon snug against his shoulder and cheek. And though Davis barely heard the shot over the loud music, he saw the flash of the weapon right before the round hit the old man square in the chest.

"No!" Davis barely heard himself yell, but it was too late.

The other nine of his men scattered and that's when Jerry dropped to the cleaned street a few feet away. He never heard the shot that killed his friend right before him. He stared as pooling blood seeped from the side of his head.

Jimi Hendrix sang on, *'There must be some way out of here, said the joker to the thief...'*

Davis stood with his boots glued to the pavement. It took everything he had not to move. He dropped his weapon to the ground a few feet away and held his hands up in surrender.

"Don't run!" he tried to shout to his men while Jimi stole his words.

They heard none of his warnings.

He watched three of the men try to scale the metal gate. He watched one try to run into the coffee shop for cover. He watched as one tried to run farther down Hemlock Street. All nine died from unheard shots coming from different directions. While every one of his men were hailed down dead, Davis held his place as the music ended with *'all along the watchtower.'*

Then silence, except for the persistence of his ringing and rushing pulse.

The bodies of his men lay strewn along the swept asphalt.

Before him, the wind off the coast blew a lock of Jerry's hair across his face. Blood still oozed, no longer at a pulse rate, from the side of his head.

Davis' hands still remained up though they shook like crazy.

After a while, his ears ceased to buzz. The shaking started from the pit of his stomach. He didn't mean to, but he glanced at dead Jerry again and something overtook him. Before he knew it, he leaned over and retched bile from his stomach. Then he was left with a dilemma as he rose and felt a string of saliva hanging from the corner of his mouth. He took the chance and wiped it on his inner shoulder. Expecting a bullet to fly through his torso any second, he jumped suddenly at the loud clang behind him.

Turning his head, he eyed the opened gateway.

It stood open, ajar a few feet wider than before.

Breathing hard, Davis looked around. There was nothing. No sign that if he moved, he'd meet his demise. No indication that if he didn't, he'd die there any second.

The flames on the other side of the gate were dying down. The black smoke billowed into the sky. Getting back to Astoria would take some time. That was if he made it through the gate to begin with.

He swallowed hard.

With his heart rate accelerating again, he took a few more breaths.

Nothing.

Just the wind now.

Despite the cold chill, sweat ran in rivers down the sides of his face into his graying stubble. It itched terribly. Davis turned in an about-face to the gate. No one shot him. A few of his dead men were piled before the exit. He took a step toward. Then another. A few more. And then he ran. He couldn't help but run faster as he reached the exit. Suspecting that they'd shoot him down at the last second, he leapt over the dead as he bolted through the opening.

4

SLOANE

"Daaamn..." Chuck said in the microphone as they watched the survivor run away. "What just happened? Are you sure we shouldn't stop him?"

"No. Let him go. That's the plan, remember? He's the messenger. We have a prisoner and a drone set to intercept," Sloane said.

"Drone?" Mae asked.

She ignored the question. Some things had to be kept secret. Even from them.

"Can I get down there now, and tend to the injured?" Kent said. His tone gave Sloane the idea that Kent wasn't fully on board with her tactics. No time for that now.

"Of course. You don't have to ask."

"I hope the old man's okay," Kent said a smidge softer than before.

"He's moving. I can see him through the camera. I thought he was going to give us away there for a second," Sloane said and then remembered everyone heard her on this frequency.

"Good job everyone. That went as well as...expected. Though I wish we didn't have to use force. They left us with no choice."

That's when she heard, "I thought you said appear weak when

you're strong. That was bat-shit crazy, Mom." Wren's voice bellowed, "And whose idea was the choice of music?"

Sloane knew this was coming from Wren. Always the opposition. The answer would surprise her, though.

"Jason's," Sloane said, letting the pause hang in the air. "Now go and help Kent. We can talk about this later."

Getting used to having everyone hear her words, even to her own family, made her abruptly end the feed. It was time to send Jason on his mission, clean up and glean all they could from the one they caught before the others returned. They needed to get ready again, and soon. It was all up to Jason now and she hoped his plan worked.

5

DAVIS

By the time he made it to the highway on foot, Davis still felt eyes upon him. Despite the coming dark, he figured they had infrared cameras housed in some of the trees he'd passed through. "They planned this from the start," he said through gritted teach. "I need a vehicle." He eyed several abandoned ones along the route. Most of them had one indication or another that they were useless to his needs. Tires blown, missing, or otherwise. He'd remembered seeing a few more as they came in.

These people, whoever they were, would never leave a useful vehicle for him to make it back to Astoria anytime soon. No, they knew what they were doing. They were buying time. They were making him pay and they'd let him go, knowing he'd return with force. Though they had no idea what they were up against. They might think they knew...but they didn't. Not really. That's what scared him more than anything. This would cause a war. One he didn't want to hang around for.

"If I could just sneak in and get my wife and the kids out before it's too late, I'd take them away and leave without a word."

A plan rose into his consciousness like a rising hot air balloon but burned and fizzled just as fast. As soon as he envisioned running with them, he knew it was too dangerous to consider fleeing. He'd already risked their lives enough. They'd never let him take her and their two young sons. Ever. No, he was trapped there. *Indentured servitude* was what they called it. He was an indentured servant. Maxwell Davis, Iraq Army veteran. The audacity. He shook his head in frustration as he continued to jog on into the early night. He felt trapped. Unworthy and really freaking tired now.

Two more years of this and Tale said they would let him take his family and leave. That was their deal. They'd offer him the choice, stay or leave, but service first. It was insane, but he held no power now.

Tale, the imposed king of Astoria, made the legendary Al Capone look like a nice guy. In the past, he'd ordered the killing of entire families for any inkling of disloyalty. As a former gang lord, Tale had escaped prison during the pandemic years after being incarcerated for multiple murders, rapes, and robberies.

Meanwhile, Davis had lost his parents and siblings to the pandemic. Just returned from war, the jolt sent him spiraling as he cared for his wife and two boys. He'd neglected to see the danger of having a drug lord taking over the small town so soon. He thought he'd had time. He thought things would improve. Things spiraled out of control too quickly and then the world essentially ended with a new set of rules to go by.

Tale was known for having a particular sadistic streak. A chill ran through Davis's spine just thinking of his crimes against humanity. It wasn't that he was afraid of the man. He was afraid of the crazy. There was a difference.

Stopping the running cadence, Davis looked to the sunset in the distance. If they were watching, he should warn them. Just in case someone still had eyes and ears on him. Looking into the darkening night, he yelled, "You don't know what you've started. Leave now. Vanish. Run for your lives while you have the time."

6

KENT

"Just pull it off," Kent said, and Wren tugged away the strong Velcro tabs holding the bulletproof vest in place as he held the old man up. "That's it. Now pull the chest frame away."

"It's heavier than I thought," Wren said, struggling with the bulletproof ballistics vest.

"Keep breathing. Deep breaths, that's it," Kent said to the old man.

"Damn…thing 'urts. Couldn't catch my breath."

"Don't try to talk. I cannot believe you agreed to this. What the hell were you thinking? A few inches north and there's no way you'd've survived a shot like that. Instant heart attack, man," Kent said.

"I wanted to. My choice," the old man said.

"Save it. You're not a martyr," Kent said and motioned for a few men to take him away to the infirmary with the stretcher. "Wren, keep an eye on him. Monitor his pulse until I get back."

"What are you gonna do?" she asked.

"I'm checking on the others," he said.

Her eyebrows lifted. "They're uh, dead, aren't they?"

"We'll see. Go on."

She nodded, he suspected knowing now, he didn't want her a witness to what he was about to do. He just needed to know. He needed to make sure they were dead. If not, he would end them himself if he had to. All but one. That was the plan.

Turning on his flashlight, he pointed the beam at the man nearby, his blood sticky on the asphalt. He was dead-dead. There was no doubting the deadness there in one glance. Sadly, he wasn't more than mid-twenties, if that. He was once someone's son, though he was on the wrong side of this mess. It was an awful world now. Even so, Kent placed his gloved fingers against the man's neck. Nothing. No thumping. No signs of life. Just an empty void. He still wanted to make sure of the finality.

"Did you check him?" Chuck asked.

He hadn't known Chuck was standing beside him. His hand jerked away from the dead man's neck.

Confused by the question, Kent said, "Well, there's no pulse, if that's what you mean."

"Nah, I mean, communication devices, weapons, any kind of information?"

Kent shook his head. "No, I didn't. He's just dead. That's all I was after. He's all yours now. Check away."

Standing up, Chuck flashed him a look. "What?"

"You don't approve of her methods, do you?"

"What do you mean?"

"You're a doctor. You took an oath, right? The Heimlich... something like that. *Do no harm*. That's what it says."

"You mean the Hippocratic Oath. Heimlich is a first aid procedure for choking, you idiot." Kent began to walk away then spun on his heel. "No. This...doesn't bother me." Though he wasn't sure why, he was raising his voice. "Her methods are unique only because they're classic and we're not dealing with a classic enemy. We're dealing with savages. And the phrase *first do no harm* does not appear in the Hippocratic oath. It never did. Keep that in mind when you piss me off."

Pointing to the market Kent said, "Have you checked on our prisoner?"

"No. Sloane said to wait for her. As far as I know he's still in there."

"You mean no one's checked to see if he's all right? That was an eight-foot-long drop."

"I'm sure we'll get to him," Chuck said. "He's not going anywhere. He's got an entire box of Twinkies with him to keep him company."

Kent left Chuck standing there to deal with the latest of the dead ones while he headed to what used to be the market. It was now only a cleverly disguised trap with Twinkie bait. Though the closer he came to the entrance, the louder the banging came from down below. Someone's small silhouette stood near the doorframe. Arms crossed. Head held high.

"Mae, what are you and Nicole doing here?" Kent asked noticing Nicole standing behind her in the dark as he approached.

"Mom said to wait until you made it over. She doesn't want anyone going down there until he's disarmed. He probably has weapons on him still."

"Well, he's sure making a lot of noise."

After he said those words, the banging ceased.

"He must have heard my voice," Kent said in a whisper. "I thought the room was sealed. There was nothing in there except for a mattress so he didn't break his neck. What's he using to bang on things? It sounded like metal."

"Duh...his gun," Mae said.

Nicole brought her hands to her mouth.

"Ah...why isn't he shooting with it then?"

She shrugged her shoulders. "Maybe he's afraid the bullet will ricochet off the sides?"

A moment later, the sound of a round striking the metal wall went off, causing both of them to jump.

"Maybe not," Mae said.

"Okay. You two go find your mom. I'll wait here."

He watched both girls run off. It was already dusk then. As soon as the sun dropped behind the clouds, the cold wind seeped into every open crevice of his jacket. He shivered with each gust. In an unsteady voice he said, "Hey. I know you can hear me. What's your name?"

There was no reply for a short time. Then a voice echoed, "Let me go. You don't understand the trouble you're in." The man grunted then as if letting out a suppressed moan.

"This will not end well for you," he strained to say.

Kent believed him. Choosing to ignore the warning, Kent said. "Look...my name's Kent. I'm a doctor. Are you injured?"

The man in the chamber let out a chuckle. "Man, I'm not telling you anything."

"You just told me we're in big trouble. By the sound of your voice I'd say you're in a lot of pain. The rest of it's not my area. I'm just here to help you," Kent said as he watched the silhouette of the woman he loved walk his way. The gun holster strapped to her thigh swung with her hips. He couldn't get over how beautiful she was or how much he'd come to love her, even in these perilous times.

Sloane must have detected his sudden lusty mood. He found her eyes smiling at him as she came out of the darkness.

She held his stare with a smirk as she neared. "Hello, Mister."

Kent held a finger quickly to his smiling lips. "He can hear everything we say. Isn't that right?" he said a little louder.

"I don't know what you're talking about," said the guy below.

Sloane nodded.

"What's your name?" she asked a little louder.

"Not giving you any information...lady."

"Fine. Stay down there," Sloane said.

"He's injured," Kent whispered.

She shook her head. "Not my area."

He was about to say something, protest for the living, when

another round went off in the chamber below them. The guy wasn't making it easy on himself.

"He may have just shot himself," said Kent.

"Still...not my problem," Sloane said and turned away.

Kent let the silence linger for a while as he watched Sloane walk away. Then he said, "Hey, I'll return in the morning. You'll be treated well. Just come out without a fight. Give us the information we need."

The wind off the shoreline gusted for a moment. The man below said nothing. Then Kent heard, "How'd you know I didn't just kill myself?"

"A man in the apocalypse with a big box of Twinkies? Nah, you have riches, my friend. You wouldn't give it all up."

"Dickhead."

"Yup. See you in the morning."

He was exhausted. The emotional highs and lows of the day took a toll. On his way back to his truck, somewhere beyond the street to the left, glowing flames caught his attention as they edged up a hill. One person stood still in his path. He soon realized it was the crazy old lady. She seemed to be staring at the same thing. "What is that?" he asked her.

"They're carrying torches up the hill."

"Why?" Though he felt he should know the answer.

The old lady turned to him, her right cheek pulled up against her eye as she gave him the stink eye. She looked at him like he was the crazy one. "That's where they're burying the dead. Doesn't she tell you anything?"

By 'she,' he supposed the old woman meant Sloane. And no, she didn't tell him everything. Only he wasn't going to admit that to the old lady. Instead, he said, "Have a good evening." Then, instead of going to his truck, he took a deep breath and set out for the line of torches meandering their way up the nearby hill like a glowing serpent. The exhaustion would have to wait.

He hustled up the path, finally catching up to them as the wet dirt slipped under his heels. The rain began to pelt with a vengeance. Grim, every one of them. That's what he saw in each raindrop-covered face. At least they weren't celebrating. Of course, carrying dead bodies over your shoulder as you marched up a muddy hill in the rain with only torchlight to see by didn't make for a happy occasion. At least he hoped not. When he reached Chuck, the first thing the man said was, "At least it was them and not us."

That statement stunned Kent. It landed in the pit of his stomach and spread like dread through his veins.

They landed the bodies on the sodden ground with reverent ease. Kent couldn't help but wonder if they would handle the bodies with such care the next time. The time after that? Or would they simply let the body weight crash to the earth with a splatter, making a crater in the mud? He had taken lives, rightfully so, on his own. He wasn't sure why he was struggling suddenly with humanity or the lack thereof.

"We have to dig the grave," Chuck yelled over the pelting rain.

It was Boyd that asked the question on Kent's mind. "One for each of them?"

Chuck was already shaking his head. Rain was coming down faster now. "No. One big grave. We don't have time for more."

That's where Kent found himself for the next hour. With dwindling torchlight, Kent grabbed a shovel from one of the others and began digging. Alongside them, they were guilty of digging a mass grave into the ground only three feet deep. Afterward, they picked up each body, one at the head, one at the feet, and laid them gently down. The worst part of all was shoveling the wet sandy loam over the faces of the lives they'd taken that morning. In death, they were not the enemy. Instead, they were men, young and old, with lives spent too soon. It affected him more than he cared to admit. Thankful for the fleeting light of the torch, the group wound their way back down the narrow path. The rain picked up. Each of them was soaked through. No one said a word. But without fail, Kent witnessed the same expression on everyone's face. They had done something bad. They'd committed this crime as a group. Willingly. Each of them, guilty of murder. As everyone dispersed, one of the women, her face cast in shock, said under her breath, or at least he imagined she did, "Why didn't we just let them go?"

He stopped in his tracks. Perhaps to comfort her? She walked past him without notice. He cast his eyes to the sodden ground, the same question rolling through his mind.

Rain was good at masking emotions. Once he made it to the cab of his truck, he closed the door with a slam. His hands were covered in dirt. He hadn't realized he was shaking from the cold, so much that even inserting the key into the ignition was a challenge. Once he turned on the engine, he realized there was a drop of rain about to drip from the tip of his nose. He wiped it away with his dirt-covered shirt sleeve. Then another formed. And then for some reason rain streamed down his cheeks as well. He wiped away the incessant moisture and drove home.

7

DAVIS

Well past the ink stain of night, Davis kept reminding himself to place one foot in front of the other. Despite his heels' raw flesh rubbing away against the backs of his leather boots, he counted himself lucky. Lucky to be alive. Even still, like times past, with his eyes wide open against the dark night sky, images of dead Jerry leaking blood from his skull flashed before his view intermittently. That and a periodic buzzing kept coming and going with the gusts of wind.

He was used to this by now. He'd served his duty to his country in Iraq. That hellhole never ceased. It was like a scab festering for eternity. Buddies died. Enemies died. Buddies died again. Their last images were seared forevermore into his memory, only to rise once again from the gray ashes to peek at Davis' current life.

He used to fight them. In vain, he'd urge the dead to stay dead...down deep, in the dark. But they refused in the end, and he wasn't surprised to have Jerry visit so soon.

"You could've fucking listened. I don't feel sorry for you."

At times he talked to them too. Hell, if they were going to bother him...he might as well get in a few good words.

The wind had picked up and with it the constant moisture common in the Northwest. He was dampened through, and even though the adrenaline flooding his system was long gone, his hands shook uncontrollably. They were numb despite his efforts to warm them in his pockets as he walked on, ignoring the pain in his heels.

Never without a weapon, he kept grabbing for the one he'd discarded to save his life back at the crazy gates of hell. "Dammit."

Then he reached behind his jacket and pulled his concealed carry weapon. In the chaos behind the gates earlier, he willed himself not to comply with his own automatic training and resisted the urge to reach for it. Had he even thought about it, he was certain he'd have a hole matching Jerry's in his head. They could be twins in the afterlife someday. That wasn't comforting. His pace quickened. He knew his family's lives were at stake.

The living ones flashed before him. His wife…he couldn't even go there. His boys were still so young. They were the only reason he still choked down air every miserable moment. Without them, he welcomed Death's sickle.

To him she was anything but a grim reaper. Nope, Death to him was a sultry seductress, forever letting him know that the pain could end here and now. From her sweet lips to his, he could let all the agony and exhaustion slip away. She was a sweetheart. He liked her. And for now, because of the living, he'd blush and say, *No, thank you…just a little while longer, darling. Someday soon…I promise.*

A few more steps on the dark road and his left boot landed on the edge where the asphalt met its mother. Correcting east, Davis instinctively widened his eyes a little more in the dark, desperately trying to seek a bit of light. With another gust of wind, came a slight buzzing in his ear.

"This is bullshit. I need to stop. All I need now is a broken leg to deal with."

Seeking the edge once again, he knew there was a ditch leading to a berm and the ever-present evergreen haven above. Though he couldn't see a damn thing, he carefully placed one foot on the soft earth and kept going at a snail's pace. The ocean, according to his damaged hearing, had descended south about an hour ago, so he was fairly certain he would not fall off the edge of a cliff. Oh well...if he did, it wasn't intentional. Not a bad way to go. Shit luck for him. Death would be smiling then.

Leading one foot after the other, he crossed the muddy ditch and felt the upward climb coming. It was an easy thing to jump a ditch and scurry up a berm in the daylight but terrifying without any light at all. Once up the berm, his hands scrambled for rocks, roots anything to grab onto. And then he was there, feeling around on the forest floor like a blind man searching for change. Just a damn tree to lean against out of the wind. That's all he was after. That and pine needles to cover himself to steal some warmth for the night. There was no short supply of those. With rough, numb hands he didn't feel the pricks as he heaped forest debris up and over his legs.

His only real fear was forest animals. Bears, cougars and moose. Yes, moose. Moose had the same reputation as hippopotamus on a safari. No one really feared hippos but piss one off and watch out. They actually killed more humans every year than lions or tigers. Same thing with moose. They were responsible for more injuries to humans than bears or cougars every year.

It was hard to tell if his eyes were open or closed after a while. He kept blinking them, not discerning any change in the darkest dark. After Jerry's image visited him once more, the red in bright contrast against the black, he pushed the grisly scene away and focused on his boys. It took an effort. He was tired. He was hungry, and the hours felt like days to get back to Astoria and to Tale...empty-handed and bereft of his crew. He knew what that meant. It was like closing your distance to the devil because he had something you wanted. Something he cherished. Beyond all measure, his sons. No matter what, he had to pull that tether to hell as fast as he could.

8

SLOANE

Sloane stood in the silent morning, staring out the cloudy window. There would be no sun today, like most days, to see as far as the ocean, not from her view. She felt his approach from behind her. For a tall man the silence of his step was surprising. "Good morning."

"Same to you," Kent said.

"I didn't sleep much at all last night."

"That makes two of us," Kent said.

She couldn't help but feel there was a distance between them now. She hoped it passed soon.

"Jason's been tracking him all night. He sent a report this morning. I hope he knows what he's doing. We're depending on his expertise. Without knowing the location of these guys we're taking unnecessary risks. It's like feeling around in a dark closet. You never know what you're going to find or what will find you first," Sloane said. Speaking her thoughts out loud, she hoped Kent would close the void. "I just wish now we'd sent someone with him. He insisted on going alone."

Kent shook his head with a blank look on his face while she talked. "I'm sure he has it under control. He's healed up remarkably since we found him. I have to run. I have what I suspect is a broken leg to deal with. Despite the mattress, our prisoner's in bad shape."

She turned away from the windows then, her eyes forming slits. "Are you upset with me because our prisoner broke his leg?"

"I'm not upset with you at all. I don't know how anyone could witness what we did yesterday and not have reservations. Hell, the music keeps replaying in my mind over and over again on a reel. I can't make it stop."

She almost chuckled. It wasn't funny. It was never funny when you had to take lives. Yet to Sloane, the entire scene played like a movie, a disturbing movie. Only she was the writer and producer. "I didn't choose the music. You can't blame me for that one."

Changing the subject, she said, "You're not going down there, in the chamber, are you? He's still armed. I thought we were waiting for him to spend all of his rounds before anyone approached."

He did that thing she hated. He nodded his chin down at her. "I'll be fine. Someone has to take care of his injuries. He's going to want pain medication, trust me. I'll barter for the gun."

"How do you know his leg's really broken?"

"Chuck radioed that he's been groaning and yelling all night, off and on. He offered to put him out of his misery for us. The guy is begging for help. He hasn't slept much at all according to the log. And...he's apparently out of Twinkies."

"Could be a ploy."

"I know the difference between agony and fooling around," Kent said with his tone raised. After a beat, he said more softly, "I think he's really in trouble. I won't know how much until I get down there." He began to walk away, then stopped short, turned to her and said, "I'm sure Jason is all right. Have faith in him. I know it's hard to delegate and not have control over everything, but sometimes you have to let people do what they do best."

He pulled her toward him, kissed the top of her head and said, "I'll see you later."

She stared after him a moment longer after he closed the door. There was something wrong there. Something she couldn't fix. Maybe it wasn't hers to fix.

He was right about one thing. She was worried about Jason. Not just about what he would discover, but what danger lay ahead of him still. Was she asking too much of the young man?

It wasn't long after he came to live with them that they discovered his abilities. At first it was all about his recovery. He's been through so much at the hands of their sadistic captor, Hyde. No one thought to ask him what he did before. Before the mayhem. Before the tsunami. Before the pandemic. Before the torture.

When he'd healed enough, he wanted to help. Before everything, Jason was a drone enthusiast. Not any drone enthusiast. He owned a drone shop in Cannon Beach. One where people flocked when they'd tired of flying kites in the blustery beach winds. Where bored teen boys on a family vacation pretended to check out the wildlife clinging to the sides of Haystack Rock but instead spied on pretty girls in swimsuits. Jason was an expert. He had equipment hidden away. It was what he was tortured for. But he never gave up the secrets. Until a few weeks ago.

It was Jason who demanded her attention one evening. Reluctant to speak, he'd found a yellow-lined pad and a pen, and began writing furiously, drawing out a sketched plan. It took her a while to understand what he'd meant. What he was after. He could speak limitedly now but rarely did. His hearing, however, was another story. He could detect some slight noises, but it had yet to return with any great acclaim. He was mostly dependent on lip reading. Even though Kent had fitted him with a found hearing device, he wouldn't use it. She could tell by the cast of his eyes to the side when Kent had handed him the box. Her concern was letting him go out on surveillance alone. How would he detect the noises he made with his own feet or someone sneaking up on him? They had tested him and found that his observance skills were good enough. He just sensed things.

She worried about him still, as if he were her own son. She'd put him in the worst possible of dangers. It would be her fault if something happened to him. Still, Jason had insisted on going alone.

Perhaps this was what also bothered Kent. Maybe he already resented her for letting Jason do his part.

The moment Jason left, part of her had left with him. *Please return to us safely*.

Still, the plan was solid. She had faith in him and his part in the whole scheme of things. But if something were to happen to Jason, no one would forgive her, especially not her daughter Wren.

9
WREN

She'd gone to find him, after what her mother had said. It wasn't that she doubted her mother's words; it was more that. She thought Jason was trying to please her mother. And if there was one thing she'd learned existing as Sloane's daughter...you couldn't please her all the time. She always made you feel like you could do just a little better if you tried just a little harder. It was infuriating. Nothing was good enough. Perhaps that's why she went to find him. She wanted to tell him not to fall for it.

Opening the door to the converted garage bedroom, she only discovered his things were gone. The blue T-shirt he hung by the window, folded in half and laid neatly over a strong line hung between his area and Chuck's, was missing. Perhaps it was all too much for him. Perhaps he thought her mother was bat-shit crazy at times, too. Maybe he wanted to get out before it was too late. She couldn't blame him. There were times when she wanted to flee, to be alone, to become someone else. To escape on her own. That wouldn't happen. Not yet anyway. The pang in her heart begged the question, *Why didn't he say goodbye to me?* They'd become friends, after all. She'd spent quiet time with him in this very room. They'd never kissed or anything like that, but once, he did hold her hand when they'd talked about the other place. The pain beyond the doors they both shared. He'd brushed the backs of his fingers against the side of her tear-stained cheek. *Why didn't he say goodbye?*

She had to find him; she had to find Jason. Only one person might know where he'd gone. That person was Mae. The one who kept track of them all.

Leaving the door open, she fled off into the night to find her little sister. As she turned to run up the street, the forest shadows cast a trick of light over her path. And as she ran, she stumbled onto who she thought was Kent by the way his silhouette blocked the starry night.

"Hey, where are you going?" the man said after he stopped himself, a little startled. She could see he reached for his sidearm.

It was Chuck's voice, though, not Kent's.

"Have you seen Jason?"

He turned his head to the side and looked down at her. "Nah, come to think of it, I haven't seen him for a while. It was a crazy day for all of us. You shouldn't be running around here at night, especially not right now. I'm sure he'll turn up."

Sweat beaded on the palms of her hands. She rubbed them on the sides of her thighs. "You're right. I'll get back to the house," she said and turned around. She felt his footsteps coming along behind her. She heard someone making dinner upstairs in the house. It would be fish again tonight, she decided by the smell wafting down. She didn't really like the tuna surprise, they called it, but her stomach had other ideas by its grumblings.

Chuck passed her by as she reached the staircase. He was soaked through from the downpour earlier and by the looks of him in the ambient light, he'd taken to a mud puddle. "See you at dinner, then."

Chuck tipped his head at her. "I gotta clean up first. Your

mom would fillet me showing up at dinner like this. Good evening, Wren."

She liked Chuck. He was what Mae called ballsy. He challenged their mother's plans occasionally, something they rarely did. She put up with it for some reason. Chuck was a skilled worker. He was valuable. That was probably why, Wren thought as she walked up the stairs.

She made it halfway. Just enough so that Chuck wouldn't suspect she was taking off again and tell her parents. Parents? Kent was like a dad. At least he listened to her. Turning around quietly, she crept back down the stairs ever so slightly.

"I'm glad you're home, Wren. Have you seen Nicole and Mae?"

Her mother's voice came from the kitchen window above. She must have heard her on the stairs.

Her shoulders suddenly rose up to her ears. She rolled her eyes as she thought of her response. "No Mom, I haven't seen them."

"Well, can you find, them? We're about to eat dinner."

It was as if things were normal, and her mother was calling them all to the table. It was as if the world hadn't ended…and they had not just killed a small invasion…but they had done just that.

"No Mom, it's not my turn to watch my sisters."

"That wasn't a question. Please find them and tell them it's time for dinner."

"Fine. Where do you think they might be? And where is Jason, by the way?"

Her mother didn't answer right away. "I'm pretty sure they're helping in town, resetting the store. And Jason is working on something for me. He won't be with us tonight for dinner."

"What do you mean? Did you send him somewhere?"

"Wren, please just go find your sisters." And that's when the window slammed shut. End of discussion. Something was going on. She sent Jason on a mission. That had to be it. That meant Jason was in danger.

Frustration boiled up inside her chest. Wren growled. Her mother could be so infuriating. This time Wren wasn't quiet. This time she turned and ran at a good pace, hearing her own boots clomp against the damp gravel drive.

She'd run this path many times before. It didn't take long before she curved the bend into town. Now all she had to do was find Mae and then see if anyone knew what Jason was involved in. More than likely, Mae would know what happened. It was just a matter of asking her the right question.

The town looked so different now than it used to. Electric lights lighting the night had been replaced by torchlights, and she preferred the amber glow. With each gust of wind, the periodic torches lining the streets would wave this way or that. It was as if the night were alive. She calmed her breath and looked around at the people milling about. She thought how much more she liked living in Cannon Beach now. It wasn't just the town, it was what they created here. They were surviving. They were finally learning to trust again. Thinking back to the other places they called home, miles away, she remembered feeling secure but alone. Never before had she missed her friends so much. Her family was fine. Though she needed other people, too. At least now, they had others to talk to, to bond with. Like Jason. And now he was missing. She had to find him.

Just then, she saw the shaggy black fur of their dog Ace. He attached himself mostly to Mae and Nicole now. The end of Mae's ponytail flipped around the corner, followed by Nicole's shadow. She caught up to them easily and saw that they each carried heavy loads. "What are you doing here?"

Mae turned to her. Beads of sweat covered her sister's face and Ace came over to Wren and leaned into her thigh for acknowledgment. "What do you mean? I'm here helping out the town resetting things. Why aren't you helping?"

As Wren gave Ace a good scratch she said back, "I didn't know we were supposed to help."

Mae blew out a breath, lifting part of her bangs. "That's because you're so fragile." She said 'so fragile' as if she was mocking her.

"What do *you* mean?"

Mae basically let the box control-fall to the shop floor and wiped the sweat from her brow. She looked as if she were buying time. "Don't you think you could help now? Instead of running off, doing whatever it is that you do. I don't think you're fragile. I think you're lazy."

"Wait, what? I didn't know who we were supposed to help out." Suddenly her hands were on her hips. Mae was acting as if she wasn't doing anything at all.

"I'm just saying you can help out more." Her sister looked suddenly uncomfortable. It wasn't like Mae to mince words. Mae was like a word vomiter. No filter. Suddenly her sister looked as if she were trying to avoid the conversation altogether. She didn't even make eye contact with her.

"Whatever," Wren said. "Have you seen Jason?"

That's when Mae looked a little more like her old self. Her eyes darted into Wren's. She shook her head. But then, her eyes widened just a little bit. "I haven't seen him."

She was lying, and Wren knew it. "But you know something. I can tell by the look on your face. You might not have seen him, but you know where he is."

May shook her head again. "That's where you're wrong. I don't know *where* he is. And I haven't *seen* him."

Wren was suspicious, saying the three words with a deliberate pause. "You. Know. Something. Spill it. Now."

Mae let out a hot breath and rolled her eyes. "All right. He's working on something for Mom. He probably won't return for a few days."

"That's not enough. She already told me that. What do you mean?"

"I mean he's doing a job for Mom. I don't know what else to say. Think about what happened today. Think about what Jason's good at. I can't tell you more than that, but he'll be back soon."

"How do you know all of this? Do they tell you things that they don't tell me?"

"No. I just pay attention. And right now, I need to go." Mae picked the box she was hauling earlier back up again. It was too heavy for her. She could barely see over the top. And yet she still struggled to do what needed to be done. Her sister was like that. Her mother was like that. And so was Wren. They struggled at things that were too hard for them but they eventually prevailed.

"Mom wants you home for dinner, by the way," Wren said as she walked out the door.

"Wait. Where are you going?" Mae called after her as she left the building.

Wren was already putting it together. She knew what Jason was good at. She knew what he was up to now. It was her mother's doing. If something happened to him it would be her fault.

"I have something to do. I'll see you at home...later," she called to her sister. It wasn't exactly a lie; she did have something to do. And she would see her at home... soon.

If Jason could go on a mission to help them, she could too. He needed her. He could barely speak. He could barely hear. And they sent him off to track the one guy they let go. It was madness. That's what he had to be doing. He was the only one that knew how to operate the drones. She was going to find him. She was going to help. In doing so, she would show her mother that she was no longer fragile. She was at least as strong as Jason.

10

KENT

The bitter wind had increased overnight. Each footfall emitted an audible crunch as Kent walked toward the market. Taking a sip of the bitter coffee warming his left hand, the hot liquid nearly burned his lip. The steam coiled away with each gale, like an ocean wave disseminating on a hostile shoreline. "It's going to be a long day," he said himself. In his right hand, he carried along his medical kit. There would be no doubt of its use today.

It was Chuck that he saw standing by the entrance to the market. "How the hell did you get here so fast?"

"Man, I was so tired when I got back, I skipped dinner and went right to sleep. Then I woke early and thought I'd better check on our subterranean friend," said Chuck. He notched his chin toward Kent's bag.

"Are you ready for this today?" Chuck said.

"Remember, he can hear everything we say," Kent cautioned, then took another sip of his now lukewarm coffee. "Damn, it's cold this morning."

Chuck nodded. "I know. We've already had a little chat."

"Oh yeah?" With his voice a little louder Kent said, "Did you find out what his name is yet?"

"Nah, he wants to keep that to himself."

Kent downed the remains of his cold coffee and was about to say something else when. from below, they heard, "I just really need some painkillers. An anti-inflammatory will do, anything. You guys have no reason to know my name."

"That's where you're wrong," Chuck said.

"I think I pissed myself, I'm shaking, and I'm in a lot of fucking pain. Can't you have some compassion?"

"I don't think you guys came here with compassion on your minds yesterday," Chuck laughed and was about to say something else, but Kent raised his hand and cut him off.

Wadding up his paper cup, Kent tossed it to the side into the formed trash heap. In thought, he wiped his mouth with his coat sleeve. "I understand that you're struggling. But you also have to understand we're here to help you."

Chuckling sounds came from below. "Here to help me? You assholes are the ones that put me here. You've probably murdered the rest of my group by the sounds of all the craziness yesterday."

Chuck raised his hands, shaking his head at the irony of the situation, and began to protest, "You guys..." but Kent cut him off again.

"Look, I know you're scared. But if you just tell us your name, and give us the information we need, and promise not to shoot us when we open the hatch to help you, I give you my word, no harm will come to you."

"It doesn't matter, man. I already ate all the Twinkies. I've got nothing to live for. If I give you the information you need or not, they're still going to come and kill all of you. And me, too. Which also means my family dies. So, you see it doesn't matter."

"That's just the pain talking. You probably didn't sleep at all last night. Most likely you're hypothermic. Let's get you fixed up and then we can talk about the rest."

Chuck cleared his throat. "Just give us your word you'll put the gun down. Kick it to the far end of the cell. Hell, we have shitloads more Twinkies, dude. We found an abandoned Hostess truck a while back."

The man below said nothing. There was a long pause. Chuck looked up at Kent with raised eyebrows. Then the sounds of the man sobbing, followed by a distinctive click, sent Kent into action.

Whispering harshly, Kent said, "Open the hatch, now!"

For once Chuck didn't question him. He reached for the lever, as Kent lunged for the rifle he had slung over his shoulder. Rushing, Kent raised the scope to his eye. With his heart beating out of his chest he searched for the man in the dark as if plunging a hand into muddy water to retrieve a lost cell phone. It was almost surely doomed, but he gave the best effort possible.

With everything in slow motion, Kent found the man's chest, and fired with a *whap*. The tranquilizer stuck out of his right pectoral. The small fringed flag bloomed from the inserted needle.

Holding his breath, Kent saw the gun already raised to the man's jawline.

The man's finger held the trigger, but his eyes conveyed a stunned surprise. His head slumped to the side a second later. His chin fell to his chest.

"Shit! Did you get him?" Chuck asked while wrenching the heavy lever door open the rest of the way.

"Just barely," Kent said, his hands shaking so much he had to put down the tranquilizer gun.

"How did you know he was going to do it?"

Kent shook his head. "All his Twinkies were gone," he said, shrugging his shoulders.

Chuck knelt down and grabbed the edge. "Well, look at that; he did eat all the Twinkies. And Jesus, he also pissed his pants. He's at least honest."

"Let's just get him out of there. We'll fix him up, and then see what he can do to help us."

"What if he won't? Help us, I mean. What are you going to do to change his mind?" Chuck asked.

Kent sat on his knees and looked at Chuck. "What changed your mind? You were in a similar position not too long ago."

Chuck sat up and leaned his head to the side a bit.

"Okay, I mean after I rescued you from the old man."

Chuck shrugged his shoulders. "You guys gave me a job to do. You gave me something to live for. You gave me a reason to fight the bastards."

"Same thing here, then."

II
DAVIS

So stiff were his legs the next morning, Davis barely moved them, though he gave it good effort. The rate at which he walked was hindered further by the numbness in his toes and hands, to the point that he stopped far too often. He'd only left last night's camp half an hour ago.

Like his mood, not only was the sky the dullest gray hue, like a dappled horse—nothing new for the Northwest—but the fog, too, was so thick he felt he needed a shovel to make any progress. He had a hard time walking through the thick stuff with any confidence that he wouldn't knock into something or someone. If he had to calculate it, he had maybe an eight-foot visibility range. "When does this crap end?" He didn't only mean the fog. He meant everything. It was all crap. Thick...gray...crap, from the moment he woke to the last second before he fell asleep from pure exhaustion since this all began, or ended...it depended on your frame of mind at the time.

Davis went to take another step when suddenly a buzzing in his ear was followed by dense white clouds spinning by his head. "I'd better sit down. I must be a bit dehydrated." He wobbled on his feet, crouched down and sat his ass hard on the cold damp asphalt.

He hadn't taken his boots off the night before, knowing that would allow the swelling to take over. He didn't want to try and shove a balloon up a tight sphincter. It sounded like a bad idea last night. Now he wasn't so sure he'd made the right decision. As he sat there on the road, he clearly saw the back fabric of his jump boots was soaked with blood. Much of it was brown and oxidized. There were new spots too, vibrant and rusty. "Dammit, I wish I hadn't seen that," he said, because before that he had been able to put the pain out of his mind. Now it was right before him. And it burned like hell.

"Got to get these damn things off." He quickly unlaced each boot, letting the pressure inside subside a little. Then, taking three quick breaths, he loosened the left one, braced himself and pulled steadily. The pain would've brought him to his knees had he not already been on his ass. As it was, white sparks shot through his vision. A moan escaped his lips as he peeled off the bloodstained white crew sock. He took a few more breaths and avoided looking at the damage just yet. Taking another deep breath, before he changed his mind, he reached for his right boot, and did the same thing. He wasn't ashamed that he nearly cried. It hurt like hell. Had his young sons been there as a witness to his turmoil, he could not have shielded them from his misery. By then his hands trembled as he dropped the last boot on the ground, where it toppled to its side. Davis laid his wrists on the top of his knees. He took a moment to calm his pounding heartbeat. Then after a while he peeked at the actual damage. That was the first time he really got a good look at his heels from behind. In somewhat identical red blood triangles, they were bereft of skin from the top of his Achilles tendon to the base of his foot. The brown skin had worn away, leaving what looked like exposed red muscle tissue.

Now his feet burned so much even his calves shook with the pain. "What a dumbass," he said to himself through gritted teeth. Even through the pain he couldn't excuse his own self-care negligence. He was a soldier, after all. A trained one. One all too familiar with foot injuries. He knew to minimize friction around his feet. But that was the last thing he thought of as he fled the crazy gates of hell the day before. Now he felt lame. And that was the last thing any soldier wanted to be. It was a recruit mistake.

Glancing at the bloody white cotton crew socks piled to the side, he said, "That's what you get. Wool, man, always wear wool socks." Though in the apocalypse you get what you get or nothing at all. And wool socks were hard to come by. Hell, the cotton ones were in short supply. Still, he knew better. And now he was going to pay the price.

Davis hung his head down between his knees. He knew better than to go barefoot. He knew better than a lot of things that he'd done lately. "Get a grip, man." It was an encouraging plea in self-talk. Taking two more controlled breaths, Davis sat up, pulled the knife from his side, and grabbed his left boot. As he began cutting, he said "I hate to do this, but it's not like I can go barefoot. Not for long anyway." He made long incisions from the top of the back of his boot all the way down to the heel. He was left with a long flap that he cut away too. He flexed the piece in his hands, not sure what use it might have now, and sat it to the side but would take it with him. "Okay you bastard, let's try this." Carefully stuffing his left foot inside the boot, he checked to make sure the cut edges were clear of his injury. "Not too bad." With a few more adjustments he whittled down the edges and tried the fit again, making sure they were clear of the injury. He then modified the straps of his boot to adjust around his calf. There would be a little rubbing there, but it was better than the alternative. Once he completed the other boot he tried standing. He couldn't help groaning in pain as the skin flexed and pulled. "I got to find some supplies. We can't let this get worse. It'll easily get infected. That's all I need." He trudged on then and yet he still continued to hear a slight buzzing sound in the distance. "Coffee... that's what it is, freaking caffeine withdrawals. Wish I had my pack, dammit," he said and trudged on into the thickening haze.

12

JASON

The still-warm battery pack lay in his bare hands. His eyes lingered on the black plastic casing as the warmth spent in the cold wind. The chill blew across the tops of his fingers. The warmth ran beneath. The contrast in those opposing forces was like night and day, before and after, the end and the beginning.

The man he pursued had dropped into a ravine last night and climbed out again onto the road on his hands and knees that morning. He'd strained to a standing position and moved with stiff strides once erect. Erect being a loose term, as his back bent over as he shuffled along. He had to be in a lot of pain. That's what Jason determined early on. He felt sorry for him. From his drone camera view he could tell he still struggled. This wasn't just a morning stiffness for old men. Though he had sympathy for him, that wasn't his job. His mission was to follow him back to where he came from. Find their home base. And to do that he needed to remain impartial to the man's plight. The irony was, he wondered if that's the same feeling his captors had had for him. Did Boyd feel he had to remain impartial when he was one of the guards? He knew the other young man in the group held a certain amount of guilt. He wore it like a veil. The survivors...they made him wear it, each and every day.

If Jason were discovered by the man he followed, he had no doubt the man would kill him without a second's remorse. He came from them. He worked for them. He was one of them. That's what Jason reminded himself of when he saw him lying in the road.

Boyd's plight was different, he reminded himself. He was as much a victim as the rest of them.

With each spent battery, he risked losing him again. With each recharge, he had to recall the drone quickly, replace the battery pack, and return to the last known location. There was always a risk that the man would figure out he was being used to find the enemy's location and would attempt to evade him. He couldn't let that happen. Though the rotors were quiet, they did emit some noise.

Meanwhile, as the drone caught up, Jason followed at a distance, keeping the drone from edging too close to the man to avoid detection. It was a pain in the thick fog. A long-distance game of hide and seek.

Keeping up with him wasn't easy, either. Not only that, Jason also carried a backpack full of provisions, heavy replacement batteries and a solar charger, not doing him any favors without sunlight. With enough batteries to get him there, he had to be sure not to overextend them, or else he'd lose the man. His only other option was to scavenge more batteries, which meant risking his discovery.

Chances. He was taking chances. There was a time when he'd never thought he'd have the guts to do this. It was the generosity of strangers that aided his bravery now. He owed them. He owed them his life. They gave him purpose. And this was the one thing he could do to repay them.

He was reminded when strange things started happening, once he set out on this mission. He was alone once again. For once he didn't like it. He never sought the company of strangers. He found comfort in his own space, his own mind and music. Though he found himself missing Kent and Sloane, most of all he missed Wren. His head bobbed with thoughts of her in tune to *Are You Gonna Be My Girl by Jet* as it played through his mind. They'd become good friends. He hoped for more than that someday. He missed the sight of her but more so, the smell of her when she lingered too close to him. But that could wait for now. Heck, he even missed his roommate, Chuck.

He'd always been somewhat of a loner. His drone shop and music kept him company. Now that his senses were ripped from him, he'd noticed that music still played a large part in his life. The songs he remembered often came to him, strumming through his mind at the right times along with his thoughts. Soon his pace had slowed. When he felt a rock under his boot skid, he realized it must've made a noise though he didn't hear it. He looked around, constantly aware. The lack of one sense necessitated the heightened use of others. He was drifting again. Remembering her face. The shy smile he saw every now and again when his eyes lingered on her for a little too long. She pretended to hide it, but the rosy hue of her cheeks betrayed her.

Back to work, he said to himself with an internal growl. He cleared his throat as he knelt down to click a battery pack into the drone. Focusing, he took a step back, raised the controller, watched the screen, and sent the drone upward and out again to its prey.

He walked at a steady pace and occasionally checked the screen as he drove the drone after the man's last known location. Last he saw the guy, he was having a hell of a time cutting out the backs of his boots. That would buy Jason a few moments to recall the drone. Just enough time to replace the battery pack. And luckily, the man would move slower today with heel injuries like the ones he saw.

As Jason walked, he pulled out a trail bar, tore the top of the package open with his teeth, and thoroughly munched his breakfast. Sadly, he doubted the man had any rations with him. Karma, thought Jason, was the great equalizer. It wasn't too long ago when Jason himself was left in the woods to starve. Food was the only thing he could think about. The incessant hunger made him into a kind of wild animal. Deranged and feral. Curious, he flipped the package around, wondering what the expiration date might be on the bar he currently consumed. At best, the food had expired a year or two before, but he couldn't really taste it anyway. It was only about nutrition.

With thick fog, Jason knew he would have to close the distance further to keep track of the man sufficiently. That made him a little uncomfortable, though he had no choice. It wasn't an option to lose him. That would mean letting everyone down. Letting Sloane down. They needed this information. Taking small bites of the trail bar, he maneuvered the morsels down his throat carefully, and then stuffed the bar into his pocket with his right hand and reached for his water. Eating was still a slow process, but he'd formed a routine for the necessary movements. It wasn't enjoyable yet, but he was overcoming the difficulties. And like Kent told him, some of his tastes were returning slowly now that the infection was gone. His hearing, too, had revealed a world a little less silent.

There were times in the recent past when he knew death was certain as one miserable day rolled into the next. Now he wasn't so sure.

Shaking his head to rid himself of flooding memories, Jason returned his attention to the drone controller in his hands. When he finally spotted his target, he kept his distance. The fog barely cleared at all, so there was no way to know what lay ahead. The man still walked at a slow pace, trudging along in obvious pain, swinging his arms out to aid his step. It was going to be a long day.

Taking a second, Jason scanned his periphery once again. He'd gotten used to this. Especially now that he was alone, his lack of hearing almost made him feel paranoid. Perhaps he was the one watched, instead of the other way around.

13

SLOANE

For an hour Sloane gave out orders as she walked through the streets. It was damp and cold like any other day. Members of the town seemed to show up bright and early and ready to go. There were few words spent on motivation now, especially after Astoria came to attack them. They knew the danger truly existed. They were ready. They fought back. They would have to fight back again.

Chuck already had the gate open. He'd already hauled off one of three burned-out vehicles blocking the entrance. So much had happened here the morning before. It was hard not to envision the scene all over again.

"You're doing great," she said.

He hadn't expected to find her standing there watching him. She could tell by the way he stood up quickly, as if caught unaware. Despite a cold chill in the air, Chuck had a light sheen of sweat dampening his shirt already. "Do you think we need to leave one of these in the way as a message?" he asked.

She hadn't thought about that yet. And though she barely got along with Chuck, his constant banter kept her thinking. That was a good thing. She didn't feel threatened by him. He just had a rough demeanor. "We could do that," she said, nodding her head, "but it would limit one of our escape routes if we were pressed for time."

He scratched his sweaty scalp with one finger. "True. What if we left these along the road in three different noticeable areas as a deterrent?"

"That's a good idea," she conceded and turned to leave, then stopped. "Chuck, when you get the notion to hang dead bodies on spikes outside the gates, don't bother asking me. The answer is no."

"Aw, come on," Chuck whined.

She was only partly joking. Even those barbaric thoughts would come if they didn't bring the war to the enemy. Especially if they were to lose anyone.

"Hey, by the way," Chuck yelled, "Your... Kent, whatever he is to you, saved that guy's life this morning."

She turned around. "What do you mean?"

"The prisoner. He nearly offed himself inside the cell this morning. Kent called it just in time."

Her heart might have skipped a beat, but she didn't have time to confirm it. "Is... everyone okay? No injuries?"

"Oh yeah, no one got hurt. Well, Kent shot him in the chest with a tranquilizer before he could do the deed. I'm sure that didn't feel very good."

"Thanks," she said, shaking. "I didn't know."

He shrugged his shoulders, "It just happened about an hour ago. I'm sure he hasn't had time to find you yet. Oh, and by the way, Wren was looking for Jason last night. I assumed she wasn't aware of the situation and I told her I hadn't seen him. Just thought you should know she was looking for him."

"Ah... yeah, I need to talk to her about that. If you see her, please send her to me."

"Will do. It takes a village."

She was thankful he felt that way. In fact, everyone was

protective of one another, it seemed. Especially the children. They were all they had, after all. That meant more now than ever before. As she walked back to the coffee shop/infirmary, Sloane was reminded how much had changed since they'd fled there. She was once left alone with her girls to survive against the elements. Then she met Kent and that changed their world for the better. It took a while, but she began to trust again. And now she had an entire town to care for and to protect. The funny thing was, they did the same for her. They trusted her. She wasn't expecting that in return.

When she reached the infirmary, she heard a painful moaning. At first, she thought the moans were coming from the prisoner, but the voice sounded a little too familiar. Her boots clomped on the few stairs leading to the wooden porch. The groaning came in odd, pitiful sounds, like a dog mourning his lost bone. Her hand reached for the door.

"Knock it off," yelled Kent to the old man. "I don't have anything stronger than aspirin, if that's what you're after."

The complaining suddenly stopped. Kent's eyes darted to Sloane standing in the doorway. He shook his head in exasperation. "He's been doing this all morning. I'm about to give him something to yowl about."

She nearly chuckled. That wasn't like Kent. She closed the door behind her and walked over to the cot where the old man lay. "What seems to be your problem?"

Both of his arms surrounded his bare barrel chest, sporting an angry purple bruise. He began to speak but Kent cut him off.

"I don't doubt he's in some pain. He's certainly injured, but I've given him all I can. He needs to sit up or he's going to develop pneumonia lying down flat like that."

"Look," she pointed her finger at the old man, "we don't have time for games. We need you functional as fast as possible. You're also the one that helps keep track of my daughters. Right now, I don't even know where Wren is. I haven't seen her all morning. If you can holler that loud, you can sit out on the porch and ask everyone who walks by where she went off to. At least that would be a useful use of your time between meds."

He stared off into the distance. "All right. Can't give an old man a break," he muttered.

Sloan left him then. Turning her attention to Kent, she asked, "How's the prisoner? Chuck said something about you saving his life?"

Kent spoke as if he held in a long-frustrated breath and was just getting a moment to let it out. "He's in the next room. His leg *is* broken. He was out of Twinkies. He pissed himself. And he said something about being afraid for his family whether he returned or not. It seemed as if he made the decision then and there that his life held no value. I don't know exactly who our enemy is, but he rules his own soldiers with an evil grip. That might be something we need to explore."

"Have you tried to talk to him yet?"

Kent rubbed his forehead. "No, he's still out and he'll likely experience some amnesia from the tranquilizer. I did set his leg. Without x-rays, I don't know how bad it is, but I think he has a shaft fracture of the tibia."

"That sounds like a bad day."

For some reason that made Kent laugh. She was relieved to hear it.

"I doubt he planned it that way. One minute you're standing there with a box of Twinkies in a doorway, the next, the ground opens up beneath you to a void."

Ignoring the implied guilt, she asked, "How long will it take for him to recover from an injury like that?"

"Well, he's not walking anywhere anytime soon. Not even with crutches. At the minimum, four months. Might even take longer than six months. This is a major injury, Sloane."

He looked at her as if she were naïve to the frailties of broken bones. She nearly came back out with a defensive remark, one that would have them not talking to one another for days. She decided to shut that deep down. She needed him. She loved him. And whatever he was going through right now, she would let him deal with it and come to her when he was ready.

Nodding her head, she took a breath in. "We'll take one day at a time. At least it'll keep him from trying to escape. That way we can get the information we need."

He glared at her then. It wasn't what she expected. His face turned a few shades of red, his lips a thin line. She could tell he was holding back some kind of rage. Tapping his fingers on the table, he said after a moment, "I know this is important. I know we need the information. But if there's one thing you need to understand, it is that I will never allow anyone to torture him for information. I don't know if that's where you're headed, but I need to make that clear."

That deep, dark tolerant place where she stored little slights suddenly burst open like a cannon. "You really think I would do that? Is that what you think of me? Especially after what we've been through? We are bigger than that. There is no honor in torture. That's what I believe. In case you needed to know." She turned to leave. She was pissed. How dare he think that of her? Especially after what so recently had occurred. As if she were Hyde himself. Her boot heels ate the wood floor quickly as she reached for the door. That's when she felt his hand around her forearm, pulling her back.

"Sloane! Wait."

She jerked away.

He grabbed her again, this time pulling her into his chest. "Sloane, please, I didn't mean it. I didn't mean you. I can just see how quickly this can all unravel if we sink to their level."

"How dare you?" She shook her head at him. "I don't understand you. I don't understand how you can even think I'm capable of such things."

He pulled her tightly to his chest so that she could feel his hot breath on the back of her neck. Reluctantly she melted against him. Even in her anger, he had that effect on her.

"I'm sorry. I had to bury them last night. I had to put them in the ground. The ones we killed yesterday. It didn't seem to bother Chuck. But it bothers me. And I suspect these soldiers are as much victims of this leader in Astoria as we are. That's not going to be easy to fight, Sloane. That means they're desperate. That means they'll do anything to survive."

She understood now. And though those same thoughts crossed her mind too, she didn't voice them. And that was the problem. She needed to communicate better with him. He was a constant support. They'd come to love and trust one another. She needed to remember that.

The hand she used to try to pry his grip away now lay softly on his forearm. She turned around to face him in his arms. "You have to tell me what you're thinking, Kent. I cannot read your mind. If you have thoughts or reservations, I need to be the first person you confide in before you get to this point. I need to know. Otherwise this is what happens."

He shook his head, "I wasn't sure what I was thinking. I just keep seeing the dead men I helped put into a mass dirt grave. It takes me a while to process these things I guess."

"It's a different world we live in now. The things we see today, the decisions we're forced to make, were thrust upon us. We didn't choose this world, but we have to adjust and deal with it to survive."

He leaned his forehead down to meet hers. "I know, but at what costs? That's what I'm beginning to question."

"Whatever it takes to survive, short of losing ourselves in the process," she said.

He nodded then.

She still saw the pain in his eyes, but she'd lightened his burden a little. That's what they did for one another. They each took turns with enduring strength. Soon, her time would come.

14
WREN

She'd laugh. She knew this, someday she'd laugh when she thought back on this memory. However, at the moment, it wasn't funny. It was as dark as the cold cell she once occupied in the not-too-distant past. She'd slipped into the supply cupboard and grabbed one of the backpacks loaded with gear on her way out. They kept these for emergency evacuations. It was her mother's idea, of course. Always prepared. She wasn't sure what her family would discover first, that she was missing or that a backpack had vanished. It didn't matter now.

She'd been walking on highway 101 since then. It was the only road that led straight to Astoria and she was traveling it in the pitch dark now. The moonlight seemed to have chosen to stay behind with the coastline, unwilling to go on this journey with her. The wind had picked up too, or that's what she told herself. The sounds she heard in the forest lining the winding road belonged to creatures she'd rather not meet in person. They shuffled the forest floor debris around enough to make her think they were at least as big as a cougar or a bear. Nah...she didn't want to think about that now.

Calculating in her mind the last time she'd seen Jason, it was right before her mother called them into action. Right before the invaders came to them. He must've left right then, leading Wren to believe this plan had been set in place without her knowledge and even Jason had kept the secret from her. She knew he'd worked on something, but she had no idea it was this. In her opinion, it was her mother who was being reckless now. Reckless with Jason's life. With that knowledge, she had to be at least eight hours behind him. She could only try. "If I stick to the road, eventually I'll come across him. I'll go as far as I can and turn around and go back. What can she do to me now? Ground me?" Then a tingle ran up her spine. Because she thought her mother might do just that. It was a bad idea to underestimate her mother, she conceded.

Clearing her mind, she put one foot in front of the other. She trudged on through the darkness, her boots landing on the asphalt with a repetitive beat. She'd camp soon. At the same time, she knew her family would figure out she was missing. She regretted that. She regretted the pain she might bring them. But she had to do what she had to do. In the process, she'd teach them that she wasn't fragile any longer. They'd underestimated her abilities. She could be of use. This would prove to them she was capable again.

Hours later, her pace slowed. The wind had long ago carried enough moisture with it to soak her jacket and jeans. They clung to her then, pressing cold moisture against her skin like a cuddly wet eel. *Must find shelter.* She stopped, adjusted the heavy backpack on her shoulders, and looked both left and right, only finding equal darkness. Since it didn't matter, she chose to go to the left and dropped down first into the ditch and then scurried up into the forest.

"Shelter," she said to herself, having learned the importance long ago. In no time, she'd set up the one-man tent connected to her backpack. It was a simple device and would at least keep her dry through the night. She need only unpack the roll and slide in the poles. It was like sliding into a safety cocoon. Of course, she couldn't help but remember Mae saying when they'd practiced how to set them up that instead of a safety cocoon, they seemed more like a bear burrito. "Crap, Mae," she said out loud, then and now. "Do you have to do that?"

"Yes," her sister had replied. That wasn't a comforting thought and because of that she checked herself again for the rifle she kept slung over her shoulder and just for insurance the Glock, strapped to her side, that she also lifted from the cabinet on her way out of town. The extra rounds as well…she patted against the storage belt she wore around her thin waist, not trusting them inside the backpack.

"No fire tonight," she whispered to herself not wanting to risk detection. Instead she shook out two handwarmers and placed them against her core for now. Keeping herself warm was the key to survival. While inside the zippered tent, Wren pulled out the rations kept inside each backpack. Though she contemplated fasting for the rest of the day, she knew that wasn't a good idea for tonight. Instead, she opened the pack and found a freeze-dried packet of ready-made meals. She need only add water. Packets of water were included, though Wren had already placed a tarp outside to collect as much rainwater as possible for drinking the next day. For now, she'd use one of the packets to mix the meal with. "And it's going to be a cold meal for me tonight," she said to herself. Pulling out the included spork, she laid back after taking a bite of the mushy, cold, rehydrated mystery meal of the day, thinking perhaps Jason was performing the same ritual as she was now. He'd gone through her mother's training just as she had. He knew what to do. She hoped he remembered. She hoped he was well. She prayed he'd stay that way and that his tent didn't become a burrito snack for a bear.

Then, long after her meal was complete, Wren had fallen asleep in fits and starts. The wind had picked up, flapping at the tent's fabric. Wren dreamt of folding her laundry, setting her loose socks to the side, then finding out in the end, she was missing the match to two of them. They were her favorites. Ones she always grabbed first and could not understand how they'd become separated. She accused her sister Mae of pulling a prank and began tearing the room they shared apart in frustration. Wren woke with a start, sitting straight up and realizing her tent was being ravaged by the wind, causing the zipper to pull down a few inches and leaving the fabric to baffle wildly.

15

KENT

"Hey...hey, stop. You're only going to hurt yourself," he told the stranger, who kept jerking at the restraints as he came out of the effects of the tranquilizer. Trying to pull on his leg was a bad idea. Kent had splinted the leg as well as he could after setting the broken bone.

Lightly slapping the guy on the side of the face made him open his eyes. And as patients typically did, he fluttered his eyelids several times until he was able to keep them open. It was a battle he'd seen many times over. Kent let him go through the motions while he spoke encouraging words to him.

"You're safe. Try not to move. Don't pull on your leg."

Finally, the guy was able to draw his eyesight around the room, his body and then finally Kent became the target of his inquiry.

"Why? Why'd you stop me?"

"There's...there's another way. That's not the right option."

"You don't get to tell me what my options are."

"Um...I think I do. You're tied to a bed with a broken leg in enemy territory. I think I get to tell you your options."

"So I'm a prisoner then?"

"At the moment, you're an injured enemy combatant. I think prisoner would be a step up from that."

"Nice. You're the dickhead. I remember your voice now."

"And you're my patient. It's always a good idea not to insult your cook or your doctor. One can spit in your food, the other can take you out."

The guy nodded then. He even seemed somewhat amused after taking in and letting out a deep breath.

"You seem to be fixing me up at the moment. That's counterintuitive. Why is that?"

"It could go the other way just as easily. Give me a reason."

"Look...I can't help you guys. I have nothing to offer you. They're coming. They'll kill me right along with you. I have no value now. You've got to understand the only way out of this is to run, hide, vanish yourselves, now."

Kent sat back in the chair by his patient's side. He seemed sincere. Part of him quaked with fear. The other part knew they'd never run. They were done running.

"Hey, there's more than one way out of a quagmire. Tell me your name. What's your expertise for them? What harm is there in that? We're gonna die anyway, right?"

The man shook his head from side to side. In a monotone voice he said, "I'm Marvin. I'm a civil engineer. That information is not going to help either of us."

"It tells me you're useful. You have skills."

"A lot of good that did me and my family. They're either dead or will be soon."

"Why do you say that? Is your leader as heartless as that?"

He laughed then but the movement cost him. "Man, that hurts."

"Yeah, I bet it does. You're not going far anytime soon."

"The leader of Astoria...his name is Tale. Heartless doesn't begin to describe him. It's a rule. No unsponsored families. My wife...my kids...they're as good as dead."

The man set his lips in a thin line to keep in the emotions. Tears formed at the corners of his eyes. When he could talk, he said, "I've seen it happen too many times."

"Marvin, you don't look like someone who's intimidated easily. There's got to be a way to deal with this guy. You may know things you don't realize you know. We need you to cooperate with us. Can you do that? Because it sounds like, if there's a shred of hope…this is it."

The man's eyes were glossy, but Kent could tell his gears were spinning inside his head. He took a deep breath in and let it out quickly.

"There's one way…but you have to hit him hard and fast."

16

DAVIS

No one shoots at me. That thought came to Davis as he stood in the middle of a barren highway between one point and the next. That was a plus. It was the benefit of the situation. On either end of here and there, someone was always shooting at him. He was *on travel*, as they used to call it, after all. On a sort of vacation. No emails, no work, just one foot painfully in front of the other. He chuckled and then took in a pathetic breath of moist air as he straightened and stared up at the gray sky.

At least the constant drizzle had stopped. Earlier, he'd been walking through a windstorm. There was forest debris now strewn all over the roadway, more so than before. No one cleaned up this place anymore. A moose had leisurely walked through his path earlier, barely noticing humans still occupied his space, and even he carefully picked his steps through the branch-littered highway.

That's what stopped Davis for a respite. He only had a few more hours to go until he reached the bridge leading over Young's Bay, along the Columbia River. Tale occupied most of Marine Drive. That's where the majority of the port activity took place.

Ships came in and out of Portland, Seattle and Vancouver. Supplies came in and left and Tale kept track of them all. Pirate ships…he reminded himself. That's what Tale called them. He was the captain of the pirates, which made Davis a pirate.

He shook his head, disgusted. Then, with his hands on his hips, he forged ahead, only to be brought up short by the itchy, hot, searing pain in his left heel. Even stopping that little bit of time, he realized when he looked down, the swelling had increased.

"Damn," he said and knelt to loosen the ties around his calf, but when he got a better look at the wounds, he realized they were becoming infected. Road debris clung to pale yellow ooze and flaming red tissue. He didn't want to touch the abrasions with unclean hands. "Got to take care of this."

He'd passed several buildings and deserted houses along the way but thought he'd make it back in time to get first aid. He was wrong. Clearly an infection had started in the cracks of the wounds. The swelling had only increased.

Looking around, he saw a building ahead that was probably once an old garage. Davis wanted to take his boots off then and there but thought better of it and limped his way up ahead to the white cinder block building. Someone had shattered the glass to the locked front door at some point since shards littered the parking lot. Without thinking about it, Davis took out his Glock and carefully approached the door, glass crunching under his boot heels.

He peered through the broken window of the entrance door. There were no signs of life, other than small animal tracks left in the dust- and litter-covered concrete floor. With his jacket-covered elbow, Davis punched through the rest of the glass shards of the window frame and then, reaching down through the opening, he unlocked the door from the inside. And had to shove the door inward against blocking debris enough to fit through.

With his training in battlefield first aid kicking in, Davis scanned the walls of the old garage for the expected red square with the white cross. Most garages were fitted with such devices. Accidents happened to the working man often. "Has to be here somewhere."

Taking a few more steps amongst the litter, Davis was guarded of anything touching his wounds. With careful steps he eyed what looked like the door to the office and headed in that direction with slow, deliberate paces. From the smell of the place a raccoon family or two had used the garage as a communal restroom. He had no doubt he was taking more chances with his open wounds.

When he reached the doorway, Davis saw on the wall the first aid case he was looking for. Unfortunately, it looked as if it had succumbed to flood damage along with everything else. Still, he took the chance to move over an upended desk and chair to reach the case, hoping there was something useful inside. As he tried to figure out the best way to pull the case from the wall, he suddenly heard something shifting in the debris behind him. He shifted quickly to pull his weapon, only to back into a wooden crate with the backs of his heels. Searing pain shot through him as he whipped around, only to see a something brown skitter from one pile of debris to the next. Whatever it was, it was bigger than a rat but smaller than a raccoon. "Son of a..." he said, bending over in pain. With a low growl, Davis stood again and after he put the Glock away, he ripped the first aid kit from the wall and went back the way he came. This time when the animal shuffled through debris, he was too pissed off to care.

Outside he limped to a nearby stone step and sat down. As he did, the buzzing in his head came to him again. "Dammit, I need to eat something." He briefly contemplated the building again, with the little furry animal inside. "Nah," he said to himself. "I can make it back in time."

He sat the kit on his lap and looked at the lid. "Damn, this thing's old." Opening the rusted latch, he saw what he suspected earlier was true. He nearly threw the entire thing to the side rather than look through it but instead, he took a breath. Most of the supplies inside were worthless at first glance. He began throwing out all the useless bandages and gauze tape. They were soaked through with flood water long ago and dried out. So too, were the packets of fever reducers and anti-inflammatories. He knew he wouldn't be that lucky. The pills inside had disintegrated long ago. A few plastic-enclosed bee sting swabs looked usable, as well as the poison ivy ointment. There was a liquid ice pack that would have been nice, but it too was unusable without a way to chill it. Then there were paper-covered scissors and tweezers. He could tell from the start they were useless since the rust outline on the packaging was a dead giveaway. Still, he ripped open the damaged packaging and, brushed them off and pocketed those items. You never knew when things like that would come in handy. There was one thing he'd hoped for in the kit but now he realized it might be too old to contain. Was it too much to ask for a few sealed tubes of antibiotic ointment? Then, he couldn't contain himself. He flung what was left to the side. The metal case landed with a racket and Davis found himself doing something he rarely did. He lost his cool and yelled at the top of his lungs for a good ten seconds or more. Then he hung his head between his knees and cried. That's when in his mind he saw those that died just a day before, again. Dead Jerry and the others. Then the unmistakable image of his sister, cast in blue, floated by too...followed by a young boy... "Fuck," he said casting away the images. Standing, he told himself, "Get your shit together, man. That's not going to happen," and he wiped the tears and strings of snot from his face with a swipe of his sleeve. Then he turned his head slightly to the left when he heard the buzzing again, only this time he realized it wasn't *in* his head.

17

JASON

Another glance through the screen and Jason thought he'd lost his objective. What if he went through the back door? Even as the thought came to him, he maneuvered the drone to the back side of the building, though there was nothing to see. The windows were too small and too smudged or broken and he didn't dare fly too close to get a better look.

Instead, he waited outside in the tree line for what seemed like forever when he realized he needed to recall the drone for another battery switch. It was running low already but that wasn't going to happen. He had to let the drone hover and wait. If he took that chance, he knew he'd likely never find him again. In the meantime, he'd move closer himself, so that the drone had less distance to cover to get back to him. That meant endangering himself, he knew, but it was a chance he had to take.

It was taking too long, whatever the man was doing in there. Looking at the energy feed, Jason made an involuntary growl; he could tell from the vibration in his throat. He quickly looked around himself, ensuring his safety. What if someone nearby heard him? He needed to be more careful. He couldn't make mistakes like that.

He circled the building again with the drone; perhaps he decided to leave out the back entrance after all. But when Jason finally brought the drone out to the front of the building again he saw the man walking to the side of the parking lot with a worn metal case. Breathing a quiet sigh of relief, Jason drove the drone around again, farther back to conceal the slight sound.

Jason himself was only about two blocks from the man he followed. The distance wasn't far enough to comfort him. Knowing he was in danger, despite the cold, he began to sweat. Concentrating on the controls, Jason drove the drone closer to the man, he was fiddling with something, and Jason couldn't tell what it was from his view over his shoulder.

That's when the man threw the case away and began yelling like crazy.

Jason pulled back the drone and that's when he remembered the battery was nearly shot and raced the drone back to him. Only...did that just happen? He couldn't be sure, but he thought the man caught a glimpse of the drone. If he had, he'd better run.

Jason quickly grabbed his pack and darted off to the left into the tree line. Stopping within sight of the road, he realized the drone's battery light had begun flashing. He was out of time. *Okay,* he thought, trying to calm down enough to think, and turned the drone around to see if the man followed. Not finding him in the viewer, he said to himself, *I'll land you somewhere and find you later.* It wasn't a perfect plan, but it was the only option he had at the moment. The man might track the drone right to him, so he picked a large pine tree cluster and landed the machine safely. He'd have to hide out until he could surveil the drone and retrieve it when it was safe enough. That would also mean losing the man...temporarily, he hoped.

With his heart pounding through his chest, he stepped deeper into the forest for cover, but still within sight of the roadway. He crouched down low and waited.

Moments later, Jason saw him coming.

18

SLOANE

After the town was set to rights from the previous day's chaos, Sloane began to head home when she saw Ace tagging along beside Nicole and Mae's forms up ahead in her path. Catching up to them, Sloane placed her hand on Nicole's shoulder. The girl immediately looked up and pulled away, drawing herself to the other side of Mae.

"It's all right, Nicole. There's no need to feel this way. We love you. We care about you. We all make mistakes. Please don't shy away from me. We don't blame you for what happened."

Nicole didn't respond. She only studied the ground as they walked along.

Sloane realized Mae was looking at her and shrugged. She took a breath, knowing it would take more time for Nicole to come around. The guilt the girl carried had weighed heavily.

"Have either of you seen Wren?"

"I uh, saw her last night. She was asking about Jason. Funny that you ask, because as we were finishing up, just a few minutes ago, the old man asked us if we'd seen her."

"Yeah. I asked him to keep track of you guys."

They walked on in silence a few more minutes when Mae said, "Wait, Mom. When *was* the last time you saw Wren?"

Sloane stopped in her tracks, her boots skidding on the gravel-topped road. "Last evening right before dinner, when I asked her to find you. I made what we had but left before you girls got back, remember? I thought you would have seen her. I came in late last night and went straight to bed."

Mae stood there shaking her head. "I only saw her briefly right after that. But that's it."

"Okay, we're getting ahead of ourselves. She's probably at home," Sloane said but whipped out her radio anyway. "Kent, hey, have you seen Wren today?"

"No," he said, "I haven't. Chuck said he saw her last night as she was coming home. Why?"

"Mae saw her right after that when she was asking about Jason. No one's seen her since. I'm a little worried, Kent." Once she said those words, she then realized her hands were shaking like crazy.

"Boyd...ask Boyd if he's seen her. He's watching out for them."

"Actually, I put him to work today. He was resetting the store."

"Ah...we did leave quite the mess in there. Sloane, don't worry, she's probably at home. I'll be there in a few minutes to check on things, but I've got to come back and take care of this guy. His name is Marvin, by the way."

But she barely heard what Kent said. Suddenly she knew she'd screwed up. She knew Wren wasn't at home. Nor was she anywhere in town or running along the beach. She knew her daughter had gone after Jason.

Without answering his words, Sloane took off and ran for home.

"Mom, wait up!" Mae yelled but Sloane didn't stop. She ran past the post that Boyd usually occupied. She ran up the steps to the house and flung the door open. Nothing had changed. No one was there. "Wren!" she yelled out and so help her...she was suddenly cast back into the torture house, yelling her daughter's name again.

Telling herself to knock it off, she went to Wren's room and saw that nothing was amiss.

Out of breath, Mae caught up to her, "Mom...she's probably fine. What are you worried about? She's probably on the beach or something."

Whipping around face her daughter, she said, "You're worried about her yourself or you wouldn't have brought it up. You were the last one to see her. What exactly did you discuss?"

Mae shook her head. "Just about Jason. She asked where he was, what he was doing."

"What did you tell her? How would you know what Jason was doing?"

"Mom, Mom, calm down. She's around here somewhere."

"What did you say?"

"I just said he was working on something for you and that he knew a lot about drones so it probably had something to do with that...and the guy we let go yesterday."

"Oh, Jesus! She's gone after him! That's what she did."

It was Nicole that finally spoke and broke through the onslaught of panic rising up through Sloane.

"She would take a pack with her."

"What?" Mae said.

Nicole nodded. "If she was going after Jason, she would take a pack with her. Are any of them missing?"

"You're right. She's not stupid—well..." Mae said.

And then Sloane called Kent quickly.

After a few torturous minutes, Kent called her back. "Yes, Sloane, one is missing and so is one of the handguns."

"She's on her way to Astoria, then. She's going to get herself killed!"

"You should have told her," Mae yelled suddenly.

"What?"

"You should have told her what the plan was with Jason."

"It was a secret plan. It wasn't my idea to keep it quiet."

"She cares about him. You don't understand that. We keep things from her. We all do. It isn't right. She has to function just like the rest of us. You're harming her by keeping things easy on her. That's what's happened. This is your fault."

"What? This isn't my fault. We've tried our best to protect her. She's been through too much already."

Calmer, Mae said, "We know that, Mom, but that was in the past. We don't live *there* anymore."

Stunned by her daughter's wisdom, Sloane said after a moment, "All right, she's not stupid. She took a pack and she's armed. She has training and supplies. Jason's mission was to follow the man, at a distance, as far as he could to find his base location and then return. It's nine hours on foot to Astoria back when civilization existed. Now... we stay out of contact with others. She's probably still looking for him. Crap...I can't believe this is happening."

Mae stepped in front of her mother, "It is happening...now what are we going to do about it?"

19

WREN

Wren tried out various theories that might lay ahead. She could, at any moment, see Jason walking her way. In which case, he'd frown at her at first, but then eventually smile and they'd camp for the night somewhere and head back home in the morning. Or she'd find him walking in the same direction as he followed the man he hunted, and she'd join him whether he liked it or not. He needed her help. She could at least watch his back. Or she never came across him and she kept walking almost all the way to Astoria until she felt it wasn't safe. Then...she told herself, she'd turn right around and go back to Cannon Beach to face whatever punishment her mother wanted to throw at her. Whatever happened, it would happen today. She'd either find him or not, and that excited her and scared her to death at the same time.

"Knock it off, Wren," she said out loud, knowing she was speaking for her mother again. Despite it all, despite all of her mother's toughness, she knew she loved her and would do anything for her. She'd proven that.

"One foot in front of the other," she said in a clipped mantra to refocus her mind. "Keep moving...time to move on." As the cadence stomped out, she wound her way through the debris-covered highway, keeping vigilant of her surroundings. The highway kept coming like a conveyer belt beneath her boots. She'd broken stride a few times to step over large branches or fallen trees scattering the roadway. A few rusty vehicles still hung out on the sides of the roads like skeletons, their occupants having long ago taken to new destinations or one beyond. Their glass windshields mostly crunched underfoot. "Last thing I'd want to do is walk barefoot through this stuff," she muttered and that's when she suddenly caught movement up ahead. Squinting, she saw someone running toward her around the curve in the road... and it wasn't Jason.

20

KENT

They came spilling into his office, but it was too late, Kent was already tossing supplies into his truck that Chuck had refueled. Before Sloane and the girls arrived, half the town had taken action to secure the gates and to get a squad ready for a search and rescue mission.

"I'm coming with you."

He'd heard her speaking, but he had other ideas. He was pretty sure she wasn't going to like it. "You have to stay here."

"What? No," she said, dismissing him as she topped off the magazine to her Glock with a few more 9mm rounds.

"You're not going, Sloane. You have to stay here."

He'd noticed the girls standing in the doorway. It was one of the few times Mae looked at a loss for words. Her mouth even hung open slightly. He knew she was scared for her sister, but he also knew...no one really argued with her mom. Not like this.

"That's insane."

He took a step forward and held down the arm holding her weapon. He had to make this count. "You're staying here. With them," he pointed to the girls. "With the town. You're not coming with me. I'll keep you informed."

She didn't look at him. She stared at the ground. She also didn't try to raise the Glock to shoot him...yet.

"Think about it, Sloane. They need you...here. I'll be in touch."

Slowly raising her eyes to meet his, she finally said, "You can't go alone."

Breathing an inner sigh of relief, he said, "I'm not. I'm taking Marvin."

"Who's Marvin?"

"Our prisoner."

"I thought he couldn't be moved."

"We need him for this. I'll take him for insurance if needed, along with as much morphine as we have."

The old man spoke up then. "I thought you said we didn't have anything like that."

"I lied!" he yelled.

Kent walked out of the office carrying several loaded packs and tossed them into the back as Sloane followed behind him.

"Just keep me informed," she said. Her words sounded helpless to him as he watched the men load Marvin into the cab of the double truck bed. "Easy now, don't bang him around."

"You knocked him totally out," Chuck said. "He won't feel a thing."

Kent didn't even answer that. He just gave Chuck a death stare.

Right after the realization that Wren was missing and probably trying to meet up with Jason, a plan had instantly formed. What he needed to do immediately. There was no question in his mind. Before anything else, he immediately filled a syringe and walked into Marvin's room.

"Hey, I don't think I can answer..." was all Marvin had the chance to get out before Kent plunged the needle into him. "Hey, what?" Marvin said with a look of betrayal and confusion on his face.

Kent could not take the chance that he'd argue with him. They had time for that later. He'd awaken in the cab and he'd either help or hurt. It didn't matter; Kent had medication for both scenarios.

The cab door was slammed shut on the passenger side as a man sat inside.

"Aren't you taking Chuck?" Sloane asked, looking confused.

"No, I'm taking Boyd. I don't want to risk anyone else. He's volunteered. He has his own reasons. I've got to go. She's on foot. I don't know how far I can get on the highway in this truck, but I'll do whatever I can. I'll let you know. Stay linked up. Nicole, help your mom. It's time to stop this, now. You're needed," he said and pulled Sloane into him.

"I'll bring her home if I can. Sloane, don't cry, please. I can't handle that right now. Listen," he whispered in her ear, "get things ready for you and the girls. If something happens, you take them and leave here. Don't wait. Run. I love you." He kissed her quickly and without another word, he stepped into the truck, slammed the door and sped out the gate. Looking through the rearview mirror as he passed the opening, he held the vision of her and the girls. They were terrified. That was the last image he saw of them, as the gates were closed immediately behind him.

21

DAVIS

Davis was no stranger to the sound of a drone. He knew one when he heard one. What he didn't anticipate would haunt him later. Thinking the sound was in his head was a mistake he'd regret.

Suddenly he knew. If he could catch the droners...his family might survive. He just might be able to save them.

In a split-second action, there was suddenly no searing pain to deal with. Davis ran like hell after the drone to save his family. He was barefoot then, shredding the bottoms of his feet on the glass- and debris-strewn pavement. He stopped when it stopped, turned and darted into the forest. The operator could be close by or a few miles away. He had no way of knowing but there was the smallest of chances. However slim it was, he took it to save his family's life.

The drone accelerated, and Davis found himself losing speed. The distance between them lengthened. Then the damn thing stopped in midair, moved to the right, and into the forest more slowly.

Davis slowed his own pace, crouched to catch his breath with sweat dripping freely off his face. When the little machine veered into the tree line, Davis said, "Oh, no you don't," and took off again after the thing. But within the forest, he lost track of the machine. It was nowhere to be found.

"He's got to be close by. He's hiding it." Scurrying back to the road, Davis picked up speed again and continued his relentless pace. A bend in the road came into view and once he curved around...he saw someone in the distance.

Never before had Davis wanted something so badly. Not in wars in foreign lands, not on his own soil. That person, whoever he was, held value like none other. But the closer he came into view, he realized the person wasn't a he...the damn drone operator was a woman...a young woman...a teenager, maybe. It didn't matter to him. She was the commodity he needed to save his family. Her life meant nothing to him.

22

JASON

The man ran past him. Jason slunk farther into the forest cover. *He's looking for me.* Without hearing his own movements, Jason carefully picked his way through the foliage. The drone was concealed. It could wait. The man would eventually give up and come back this way. He might even search through the forest between here and there.

I'll go ahead of him...that's what I'll do, but I've got to get the drone first.

And without any more time thinking about all the potential risks, Jason resisted the urge to run for the drone and instead carefully maneuvered each step closer to the drone's resting place. Impeded by the effort to avoid the noise-making twigs and leaves, he crouched to keep out of sight. Between glances to ensure his footing, he kept his eyes watchful of any movements near the roadway. Then he neared the drone's landing but didn't see the machine yet. Pushing away a fern, he discovered where he placed the machine was sloped on a bed of pine needles. Oh crap. Pushing away a few branches, he leaned over the embankment and saw the machine lying on its side about eleven feet downhill. With a quick glance to the road again, Jason lowered his legs down into the small gully to retrieve the fallen drone. It would take longer than he'd like but there was no way around the problem. He had to get the damn thing and get going before the man came back.

Carefully, with each hand and foot placement, Jason slipped down on the avalanche of desiccated pine needles to get the drone. He could see why the drone's slight weight caused the cascade. Even with Jason's weight, once you started, it was like riding a wave; you couldn't stop the descent. His boots finally stabilized, Jason reached down to pick up one foot of the drone and then he was left to deal with the predicament of how to get back up.

Brushing away as much of the pine needles as possible to reach some form of solid earth to grab onto, Jason pulled himself up with his left hand grasping a pine tree root. *I'm making too much noise. He's going to find me.*

But that's not what happened. Instead, Jason surfaced to the top of the gully. Placing the drone first onto safer ground, he pulled himself up and out while watching the roadway.

Maybe he already came by?

Then...suddenly, Jason crouched to the ground. At first, he thought he might have been shot. Something cut through the air with frightening speed. Never before had he wished his hearing were returned to him fully. After grabbing the drone, he looked around and saw no one. Then he turned and was about to run when he heard...something. *What's happening?*

Instead of running, Jason edged himself closer to the roadway to get a glimpse and took refuge behind a large pine tree trunk.

After a moment, the drone slid from his hand to the forest floor.

23

SLOANE

She did what Kent wanted. She prepared herself and the girls to flee if needed. They knew it too. They watched her go through the little house like a hurricane.

Mae stood in her way and shook her head. "We have a whole cache house out there. I know we do. I helped you stock it months ago like this one. Why are you wasting your time doing this now? We just have to leave if we need to."

"Mae, I can't explain everything to you. I'm doing what I need to do for us. Now please, just let me work on this while you and Nicole handle the radios."

Standing still before her, Mae held her arm out. "But Chuck is waiting for you. He wants to know our next move. They depend on you, Mom."

"I can't! I can't do leader right now…I can only do freaked-out-mom right now. They're going to have to understand that."

Her daughter donned a calm demeanor and said, "What? You quit? Mom, you're better than this. Kent will find her. He'll do the same thing he did last time. He'll bring her back. Have faith in him."

She wanted to believe her daughter. Truly. But dammit, she

was too realistic. Lucky once...if you want to call it that, but twice...no.

"Mom."

"Mae, just go tell Chuck to handle things. I have some preparation to do for now. I'm sure he'll do a good job for now. I just need a few hours."

Mae said, "That's crap, Mom. And you know it! They need *you!* Not Chuck. Not that he's not a nice person."

Her unflappable daughter had lost patience with her then. Her face turned a crimson shade as her chest heaved.

"Sloane?"

Somewhere in Sloane's mind, she heard Nicole call her name but at the moment, she could only stare at Mae seething at her. In reality, she was preparing for Wren's death. The inevitable. She knew it would happen. No one was that lucky. She barely survived the first time.

"What, Nicole?" Mae answered instead as she gave her mother a disgusted stare.

"It's Kent...he's asking for Mom."

"Oh," Sloane said, breaking the contest. "What? Have you found her?" she asked.

"No...no, I don't want to you to get your hopes up. I'm just checking in. The roads this way are pretty bad but we're going as far and as fast as we can."

"Okay. We suspected that."

"Yeah," Kent said.

"How are the others?"

"Boyd's fine. He says he misses you. I haven't woken Marvin yet. I'll do that soon to gain any intel."

"That's funny about Boyd. Good one."

"I know, look. I'll get back to you as soon as I can. So far, there's no sign of her."

She nodded and found tears running down her cheeks. She

told herself to get a grip. "Okay, it's too soon. I know. Please be careful."

"Will do."

And then he was gone.

Sloane realized then that she was holding the backpack she'd been filling earlier. They already had go bags ready and Mae was right, there was an entirely stocked cache house waiting for them if needed. "Here," Sloane handed the pack to Mae and turned to the door.

"Where are you going?" Mae asked.

"You said Chuck was looking for me? That's where I'll be. Let me know the moment Kent calls back."

Mae's eyes lifted. She smiled. "Yes, Mom."

24
WREN

She stopped. Hands to her sides. Her heel taking a backward step.

The black man barreling toward her was definitely not Jason.

With molasses movements, Wren reached for her gun. Pulling it, she aimed at the man only fifty feet from her and gaining. "Stop!" she screamed.

He kept coming.

"Stooop," she screamed again. "Don't come any...!"

He kept coming.

And then her finger squeezed the trigger.

25

KENT

He hated to do it, but he had no choice. They needed him. Slapping the side of his face lightly, Kent said, "Marvin. Marvin, wake up, man."

"He keeps falling back to sleep," Boyd said.

"I know...we have to keep at it. The sedative I gave him earlier was pretty strong. I don't want him in pain. We don't need him yelling a lot or causing himself more harm."

"Was this really a good idea? What if he tries to lead us into a trap?" Boyd asked.

Kent was trying to formulate a response when they heard, "Not leading you...in trap."

Marvin was trying to open his eyes. They fluttered like crazy. The struggle was real.

"Just take it easy," Kent said. "Keep trying to wake up. I need your help."

But a second later...Marvin snored again, and they started the whole process once more.

"Keep driving," Kent said.

But when he saw that Boyd kept checking on their progress in the backseat, he said, "And watch where you're going. We don't know what's out there. I'm not just referring to the road debris."

"I know. I just hope he can help us."

But Kent knew there was more than just the location of Wren that Boyd was thinking of. Boyd volunteered for this trip for a reason. It was his chance to learn more about the enemy and the location and fate of his young sister.

Kent had reservations about taking Boyd along, but he needed someone willing to go and though Chuck offered, he needed him back in town. Boyd was the best option in a short amount of time.

"Marvin," he tried again. "Wake up, man. I wish I could sit him up without hurting him."

"He's going to be in pain no matter what you do. Hold on, I have to go over a branch here."

With a thud, Marvin sucked in a breath and let out a groan.

"Help me sit up," Marvin mumbled with his eyes closed still.

"I'm trying."

"Here, hold my arm. Pull yourself up." Kent said and steadied his forearm in front of the man for him to grab.

Marvin reached for Kent's arm but soon realized something was wrong. "Wait, you guys handcuffed me? I have a broken leg for fuck's sake."

"Doesn't matter. I can't take any chances you'll reach for my gun when I'm not looking."

Still, Marvin struggled to open his eyes as he argued with Kent. "Whatever, man," he said and used his bound hands to reach for Kent's offered arm. Then he pulled himself up in a near-sitting position, all the while groaning in pain.

"I know it hurts. If I give you more pain meds now you'll fall asleep again, and I need some answers."

The man's eyes fluttered more as Kent shoved pillows behind him, then gave him a bottle of water.

"I've already told you guys everything I know. I've got nothing to lose now. Don't you get that?"

"You might still have some information that will help us."

"Where the hell are we going?" he finally said, realizing he was traveling in a vehicle. "The last thing I remember, I was in a comfortable bed in your infirmary, not moving in a vehicle, after you guys shattered my leg."

"Yeah, something happened. Keep drinking water. Your mind will clear up in a few minutes."

Marvin guzzled the water and noticed Boyd driving. "Hey, who are you?"

"He's just Boyd. You don't need to worry about him. Listen, where exactly is Tale located? Where does he operate from in town?"

"His office."

Kent sat back on his haunches and tilted his head to the side.

"If you don't have anything to lose, then you can help us."

"What's happened? Our conversation earlier, or whenever it was because time is screwed up right now, you guys seemed pretty stable in your commitment to remain where you were. Did they find us? Are we fleeing...that's what happened, isn't it? I told you to run before. You should have listened to me then. It's too late now. You'll never survive." His eyes glassed over as he shook his head. "Not even your wives or children. None of them."

Kent held back his own emotional reaction and studied Marvin while he guzzled down more water.

Reaching for the bottle with a hand shaking from the bumps in the road, Kent said, "Take it easy on that. I can't have you choking on your own vomit."

Marvin laughed. "Yeah, what an inconvenience that would be."

"It would, Marvin. We need your help."

Marvin shook his head. "What? What the hell can I do?"

Kent cleared his throat. "If you look around, you'll notice we're on the road *to* Astoria. Not away from."

"I'm not even from here; it all looks the same to me. Why the hell are we heading there? You'd better have some big-ass army with you, and a couple of nukes. As far as I can tell, it's only us bumbling around out here on this road."

"We're not exactly going there. We let one of your guys go so that we could track him back to your camp. The problem is, one of our teenage girls ran away to track the tracker, if that makes any sense to you."

Marvin held his hand up. "Wait a minute, wait a minute. This is all due to teenage drama? You guys have your priorities out of whack, my friend. I'd call that cleansing the gene pool. She's not going to survive if they get hold of her. Count on that."

"It's not up to you to decide what we do."

Marvin stifled a painful groan as the vehicle veered too hard to the left.

"Hey, take it easy Boyd," Kent said.

"Yeah, Boyd," Marvin added with gritted teeth and a sharp eye.

Kent thought perhaps Boyd took that bump on purpose; he'd managed to avoid the worst of them so far. With the unknown fate of his little sister on his mind, Kent couldn't blame him.

"There was a tree... This isn't as easy as it looks and it's getting worse up ahead. I doubt we'll be able to keep going like this for much longer," Boyd said but stared straight ahead.

"Look, there's not a lot of sunlight left. We need to get as far as we can in the vehicle and find her if at all possible," Kent said, but when he looked at Marvin, he found the man studying him.

"It's not that you need information from me. That's not what all this is about, is it? You're hoping if they capture her, you can ransom me for her. That's why I'm here, isn't it? I have bad news for you. I can tell you, it won't work."

"What if she found Jason and they're perfectly fine?" Boyd said.

That scenario hadn't crossed Kent's mind. It was a possibility.

"Yeah kid, and the power's going to come back on at any moment. Keep living the dream. Let me keep it simple for you. My team didn't return on time. Which pissed them off. They killed our families and they're sending someone to kill you. That's the reality. I'm as good as dead and so is the guy you're tracking. Which one was it, anyway? Jerry? I bet it was Jerry. He can run like a weasel, little bastard."

Kent just kept shaking his head. "We don't...we don't know his name."

"You killed the rest of 'em, though?"

Nodding now, he replied, "Yes, we did."

It took him a minute, but Marvin replied, "They got off easy."

"Kent."

It was Boyd calling him. "You need to see this."

26

DAVIS

She shot him.

He'd been shot with a 9mm before. It felt like a bee sting, a slight tug on his left shoulder, but he kept going. Not once did he consider slowing down. The more adrenaline he had in his system, the better.

She aimed again.

He plowed right into her, throwing her to the hard ground. The gun went sprawling feet away, clattering against a discarded, rusted fender.

She struggled immediately and when he got a good look at her face, inside, he died a little. She was just a kid. Pushing that aside, he pinned her down easily. She'd landed on her backpack and looked like a toppled turtle.

The screams. She clawed at his face with her hands and then when she realized he didn't have shoes on, she landed her boot heels hard against his feet.

"Stop. Stop it now," he yelled.

She didn't. Her dark brown hair slung wildly around against the asphalt as she fought him.

He had hold of her jacket, just below the lapels. She lunged for the gun, too far away, and because he thought she might get lucky, he yanked her up to a standing position.

"Stop! I mean it. I'll punch you in the face if you don't. Last warning!"

The girl used the strength in her legs to spring up and jump onto his bare feet with her boots. He guessed her goal was to free his grasp on her. But that wasn't going to happen. She was the ticket to his family's life. Searing white pain went through him on impact but he kept hold of her despite the now very painful wound in his shoulder.

He screamed and growled and then tried to catch his breath. In the meantime, he grabbed her by the hair to keep hold of her, turned her around and thrust his right arm under her neck, squeezing tightly. She didn't weigh much more than a ham sandwich, and he hated her damn large lugged boots, but she was springy. He'd give her that. As he tried to calm his breath, so he could see straight, she tried to bite his arm. Tighter then. He squeezed. Then she was doing her best to pull his arm away to make room to suck in some air. When all else fails, give them something to do...like gasp for breath. He knew she was fading. He'd have to be careful there. He didn't know his own strength at times, especially now.

Pulling her forward, he let her suck some air into her lungs. She choked on the freedom he allowed as he yanked the backpack off her. "Slow breaths or you'll pass out."

Slinging the pack over his other arm, he held her in a choke hold again, lighter this time, and pushed her the way he'd come.

Even though she was wearing down, she tried to kick him, bite him, do anything to get away from him. He thought, *Good...you're going to need to fight where you're going.*

27

JASON

Stunned, he could not believe his eyes.

She screamed in terror, her mouth wide, her face blood red. The man hauled her past his position. The terror on her face suddenly matched the anger within him. He should have hidden away but he was too stunned to see Wren...let alone in the man's arms, kicking and fighting back. *What is she doing here?*

Each time she gained pay dirt, the man squeezed a little tighter around her neck. The man never noticed him standing there, in the tree line, as he passed by with his prey.

Please move away from him, Wren. Jason automatically pulled the handgun he carried and aimed. *I might hit her. The bullet could pass through him or I could miss.* He couldn't take the chance of hitting her, too. Instead, his hand shook with the anger rising within him.

Stop...

Think...

Away, away, he's hauling Wren away.

Jason crouched low, out of sight, watching, looking for an opening. The beast's hands were full of her, his left arm around her throat and his right underneath her breasts. With each step he increased the distance, shoving her legs forward with his own, stealing her away. He was going to hurt her. Jason couldn't let that happen. Not again. Without taking his eyes from them, Jason fished around in his pack for the radio and quickly sent a message.

The man was distracted with his prey for now. Grabbing the drone absently, Jason haunted after them within the trees. Never the aggressor, he suddenly heard, *Savior by Rise Against,* within his mind. He was a changed man in an instant.

28

SLOANE

A little bit of crazy. It was an attribute she knew she contained. Her first husband coined the term. She lost it every once in a while. Then she was good for months on end, years even. It wasn't common. She'd never been a high maintenance kind of gal, but every now and then, she regrettably lost patience with the world, though typically she was known for her nerves-of-steel demeanor. Brushing off the scene at home, she breathed deeply, lowered her chin as she saw the crowd around the coffee shop deep in talk, and walked with determination.

"Sloane...we're sorry about Wren..."

She held up a hand. "Not now. We have that covered as best we can. Right now, we have a few scenarios to deal with. I need ballistics. Yes, Chuck, I know that's you. Who else? Who knows Astoria's layout? Raise your hands." She nodded. "We've got work to do. Chuck, I need you and any weapons specialists, engineers, and anyone with knowledge of the streets and harbors of Astoria."

"On it," Chuck said.

The old man closed one cup of the headphone over his ear.

His lips were moving. Sloane noticed he was in a conversation with someone.

"Do you think..." Chuck began to say but Sloane cut him off with her hand and walked over to the old man.

"What's going on?" she asked him.

He didn't answer right away. Instead, he looked at her with a kind of dread that sank to the bottom of her stomach. It was bad news. There was no doubt about that.

"What? Tell me," she demanded.

"Sloane, Nicole sent a message. It's from Jason."

29

WREN

There's no air. I can't breathe. He's killing me. God, please...please help me.

"Stop fighting me," he yelled at her again.

But she would never stop, never. Not in a million years. That wasn't a part of her, not now or ever again. *My gun—it's gone. But what do I have?*

Waterlogged vision prevented her from seeing much. Her best assets were the hard heels of her boots, her bare hands and her teeth for biting the hell out of him. She'd tried everything she could to get away from him, including nailing him in the face with the back of her head. He was three times her size at least, and all muscle at that. He surrounded her with his arms and chest, hauling her forward like a rag doll. Hitting and kicking him didn't work. She just wasn't strong enough. He was too large and seemed to anticipate her moves. The sweat and smell of him made her gag as it was. Manhandling her into his chest didn't make it any better.

Choking...choking for air. Her eyes were so watery, she couldn't see at all now. *Please, help me...someone.*

Wedging her lower jaw far enough beneath his forearm again, she bit down with all her strength.

"Oww, fuck!" he screamed.

Then, like before, he jerked her, repositioning his arm quickly into the crook beneath her jaw, and squeezed harder.

Oh my God, they're going to find me this way. He's going to kill me, and my mother will see my lifeless body. I'm going to die.

Darkness faded in from the sides. With her eyes wide open, pooled in tears, her vision ceased, and her ears filled with a buzzing sound.

30

KENT

"That's as far as we're going for now. We have a chainsaw in the back. We'll have to cut the tree in two and hook chains over one end and haul it back. We'll get through then," Boyd said.

"Yeah, I'd love to help you guys but...not really, I'm lying," Marvin said.

Marvin was proving to be a smart-alecky, clever asshole. Kent had to give him that. It was the way he said things, the sarcasm dripping like a too-ripe peach in the sweltering heat of an August day. It was an unfortunate situation. Kent rather liked the guy.

"You two get started. I'll supervise from here," Marvin said as Kent emerged from the truck. "But if you don't mind, can you give me something for the pain before you go? It's getting a little intense."

Kent had no doubt that was true. He'd held off on dosing him so that he was more coherent for the questioning. The problem was, he needed to reserve the stuff as much as possible. It was true that he had morphine, but it was also true he only had so much of it.

"Yep," Kent said as he filled another syringe with clear liquid. It wasn't the pain medication.

A few seconds after Kent administered the shot, Marvin's eyes glazed over. "Wait, wait..." Marvin said when his eyes began to twitch. "You sedated me?"

Kent just nodded.

"Fucker," Marvin said before passing out.

"How many times can you do that to him?" Boyd asked.

"As many times as it takes. Let's get this..." Kent began to say but the radio alerted them there was a call coming in.

Boyd listened to the message. His dark brown eyes widened and darted to Kent.

"She wants to talk to you. Doesn't sound good," Boyd said, holding the radio out for Kent.

"Never is," he said.

31

DAVIS

The girl passed out again. He'd held her too tight, dammit. He needed her. He didn't want to kill her. He'd have to watch the asphyxiation. Keep her on the edge of light.

"Hey?" Jostling her, she didn't respond. As he held her bodyweight in his arms, he turned her around to face him. She might be faking it, he knew that, but one look at her and nope...she was unconscious. "Hey, wake up. Where's the controller to that damn drone?" he said but she didn't respond. Then, from out of nowhere, something slammed into the back of his head.

Davis dropped the girl to the ground and turned quickly to see the drone coming in for another attack. He reached up to grab the thing when he felt a sharp sting to his upper left side, not far from the last gunshot wound he'd yet to care for. Then he heard rapid footsteps on the asphalt. When he turned, a young man with blonde hair aimed and fired once more.

Davis drew his own gun and quickly fired back. At the last second, something hard hit him in the shins, causing his aim to careen away from his intended target.

He soon realized it was the girl. She'd used her backpack. She'd swung the damn thing at him.

Suddenly, he realized there were two of them. The boy was the drone operator. What use was the girl? He didn't want the responsibility of her plight weighing on him anyway. But she was all over him, trying to get his gun away. He couldn't even see the kid and wondered why he had not taken another shot at him. *It's the girl... She's in the way.* And just when he thought her a mere annoyance, she whipped out a long knife he didn't know she had and rammed it into his wounded shoulder.

Davis dropped his weapon without intending to. It clattered onto the asphalt. His left arm was in tatters and now there was a damn blade sticking out of it. He quickly pulled it out. That was when he saw the boy raise his weapon again. But quicker, Davis pulled the girl up from the street with his right arm and flipped her around, her knife now at her own throat.

"Go ahead," Davis seethed in pain as he stared into the young man's eyes. "I'll spill her blood in an instant."

Aiming into him, the boy seemed to be calculating. What was odd was he hadn't said a word yet. Typically, in situations of hostage negotiations this was where the other guy threatened something back. He'd say something like, *Let her go,* or *I'll shoot you first.* Or he'd pull one of those *I don't care* moves. *She's better off dead anyway.* But he didn't say a word. Only stood there, aiming in silence. Something was weird, and Davis didn't know what it was yet. That was bothersome. There was a fact missing. He didn't like missing facts.

Davis jutted his chin out. "Put your gun down. Nobody gets hurt."

The girl started shaking her head. Davis held her a little tighter, the blade a little sharper against her skin. He felt it odd, too, that she didn't try to say anything to the young man.

The boy suddenly flipped the gun around, pointing to the sky.

"Toss it over here," Davis said.

The boy shook his head, turned and threw the gun into the woods in the opposite direction.

"Dammit, that's not what I said." He felt something warm dripping down his wounded arm and realized it was blood trailing rivers down his arm. He swallowed the rising bile in his throat. He needed to make this quick. Two shots and a stab wound had a way of trying one's patience.

"Look, kid. I don't want the girl but one of you is coming with me. It's you or her. You make the choice. Since you operate the drones, you'll have a better chance of surviving where I'm going. She won't...not for long. Understand?"

He nodded.

The girl struggled.

Davis dropped the knife to the ground and squeezed her neck a little tighter.

32

JASON

There was never a question. He would give his life for hers any day.

Wren passed out again and the man let her slide gently to the ground, protecting her head as he laid her down. The man picked up his own weapon and then motioned for Jason to toss him his backpack. Going through it, the man found his radio. He instantly chucked it into the woods. "You won't be needing that. Oh, looky here," he said, shaking a white plastic box with a red X plastered on the front. "I've been looking for one of those. Do you have any other weapons on you?" he asked and chucked the pack back to him, near his feet. He kept the medical kit.

Jason shook his head *no*.

"Open your jacket. Lift it up. Turn around. There you go. Drop your pants...no, I'm not going to molest you. Okay, now lift your pant legs. Okay."

Jason complied with the orders.

"I swear if you try anything, I'll kill you. I don't have much time. Grab the drone and gear, and let's go."

Jason looked down at Wren lying in the road. Was she even

alive? He held two fingers to the side of his own neck and then pointed at her body.

"Wait, are you deaf?" the man said.

Jason was suddenly worried the man would shoot and kill the both of them, or take Wren instead of him. He shook his head back and forth quickly.

"Why don't you speak then?"

Jason swallowed. He'd have to draw him away from Wren before he revealed that he was mostly deaf for now. He opened his mouth and pointed within.

The horror he expected fell like a veil over the man's face. Not only that, he looked as if he might faint. The man bent over and held the gun temporarily to his knee. His arm still dripped with blood. Something else was going on here, but Jason wasn't sure what it was. "Did we do that to you? You don't have to answer. I've heard the rumors about Hyde. I guess it's true then. Go ahead. Check her pulse. She's fine. She'll wake in a few minutes," the man said as he tried catching his breath. As an afterthought he said, "Don't try anything. I don't want to kill either of you, but I will if I have to."

Jason scrambled to Wren's side and touched under her neck. Her lips were bluer a few seconds ago. As he watched her, her nostrils flared slightly with each breath. The pulse beneath her chin chugged along, slow but steady. She'd wake up any second. What the man didn't see was the knife Wren had used earlier. It lay at her side where she'd landed. Jason slid it up beneath his sleeve and when the man glanced away he pocketed the blade into the side of his jacket. They would find her. He'd made sure to leave a trail.

33

SLOANE

"He has her."

Sloane's voice was as coarse as sandpaper.

"Jason? Well, that's *good* news."

"No. The other one. The guy we let go. Jason sent a message ten minutes ago by text radio. Somehow the man we freed has Wren. You're close. You've got to run!"

"Did Jason send a location?"

"Yes. Pioneer Farm Road."

"Anything else?"

"No. The actual message was, 'He has Wren. Last location Pioneer Farm Road. I won't let him have her. Thank you for everything.'"

"That guy doesn't have much farther to go to Astoria. If he crosses Young's Bay with Wren..."

"Kent," she interrupted, "please hurry."

"I understand the urgency, but it's a little more complicated than that. The road isn't exactly cleared. We'll do what we can."

"I know."

"I'll radio back as soon as I can."

And that was it. He ended the call.

He'd nearly made her crack, but she couldn't afford that now. They had to move quickly.

"Did you tell him?"

Mae looked at her mother with the same hiked right eyebrow as her own.

"I gave him Jason's message. You have to stay here with Nicole and the others. I'll return as soon as I can."

"You're lit, Mom. I heard the conversation. Kent will bring them home. They'll return soon. You don't need to go there yourself and risk your life as well."

"Mae, when you're a mother, we'll talk about this again," Sloane said as she finished packing her bag.

Sloane reached for her daughter when she'd finished gathering the things she thought she might need, and kissed Mae on top of the head. "Keep Nicole safe and keep Ace by your side at all times. You know what to do if things get out of hand."

"I do, but I wish you wouldn't go," Mae whispered.

Sighing, Sloane said, "I wish I didn't have to. No one messes with my girls."

As she walked away, Mae yelled, "What are the wise words for this one, Mom?"

"Sun Tzu said, 'Let your plans be dark and impenetrable as night, and when you move, fall like a thunderbolt'."

"No, I meant for leaving me."

"Do as I say, not as I do."

Sloane held her hand up, knowing her daughter was smiling at that one.

34
KENT

Kent eyed the street ahead. How many more obstructions were in the way before they'd get to her and Jason, and what would they find when they got there? Two lifeless bodies sprawled in the road with gunshot wounds to the head?

Damn...he tried not to go there. It was just too easy. When was he going to stop picturing dead bodies? Those of total strangers and of those he loved and cared for the most.

"Just go over it, Boyd. Don't stop. We're wasting too much time."

"We can't. We can't go over that one," Boyd pointed out the cracked windshield.

Up ahead there was a damn tree the size of a sewer pipe in their way. Never before in his life did Kent wish he lived in Florida—Arizona, even. Most of Texas was just mesquite trees, not these behemoth pines laying scattered across the roadway. But no...his family chose the Northwest to procreate decades ago. How inconsiderate of them. "Can't we go around it? It clears up ahead at least. The forest isn't dense. Bad thing is, we're out in the open then. They could pick us off if they wanted to."

The truck wheels thunked over the far end of the large

downed treetop and then spun in the soft earth on the shoulder. For a minute there, he thought they were stuck. That was the last thing they needed, but Boyd was able to pull through this time.

"Easy," Kent said. That's when he felt someone grab his wrist.

"Hey!" He turned and found Marvin staring at him.

"Please, don't put me out again, unless it's for good."

"I can't promise you anything," Kent said. "Look, they have the girl. How far can we go before your sentries will spot us? What's the borderline? You can at least tell us that."

Marvin swallowed. The man was barely coherent.

Kent didn't like the groggy feeling either. "Come on, man. I need to know this before I risk other lives."

"They're not my sentries. Let's get that straight. Loyalties live and die by the bridge. That's pretty much it. You can pay your way with supplies beyond that, but the rest comes at a price. They're little skirmishes, like fiefdoms all along there, but cross over the bridge and you're essentially in Tale's kingdom. He doesn't give a damn what happens beyond his realm."

"Great. Will we have trouble from the others getting there?"

"No. Not likely. Not unless they recognize you as one of ours. Most of them have been wiped out. They're only a few scattered bandits with an attitude now. Nothing to really worry about."

"Hmm...that depends on your definition of worry, I suppose."

"Tale kept the best of us. He knew who the fighters were and made us offers we couldn't refuse. But a warning, my dead friend, go there and there's a price to pay."

Then Kent felt something change in the truck. It was a rumbling speed. Something other than the jagged slow pace, followed by several bumps.

"Way to go, Boyd. Ten miles per hour is definitely better than five."

"It looks clearer up ahead. Just a couple more miles to Pioneer Farm Road," Boyd said.

"Go as fast as you can," Kent said.

"What's significant about that location?" Marvin asked.

Kent didn't answer right away. He wanted to. Shaking his head, Kent said, "I don't know if I can trust you."

"Isn't that a bitch? Welcome to the apocalypse," Marvin said.

"Kent?"

"Something happened there," Kent said. "We think your leader has her. Where would he take her?"

Marvin smiled at him.

It wasn't what Kent expected. He'd said something significant and he didn't know what it was.

The smile was almost sinister. "You mean Davis? I thought you said Jerry escaped."

"Kent?"

"We don't know his name. He was your leader. Where would he take her?" Kent yelled at Marvin.

"Kent!"

"What, Boyd?" Kent yelled.

The squealing brakes made them brace and everything else in the truck shift.

When it came to a full stop, Boyd pointed out the windshield. "She's there!"

Kent couldn't believe his eyes. Wren stood there in the middle of the road, the headlights blinding her.

One moment, he was stepping from the cab of the truck, the next, it seemed to take forever to get his hands on her. He ran, of course, yelling her name. "Wren?"

Then he stood there, gazing down at her, his child in everything but blood. Her eyes barely acknowledged him. "Wren? What happened, honey? Where's Jason?" She didn't answer so Kent looked around. He looked around for a body, Jason's body.

Grabbing her by the shoulders, he could see the marks on her neck in the darkening light. "Wren, where is Jason?"

"He...took him," her raspy voice said. "He took him, instead of me. He took him, instead of me," she repeated.

Kent pulled her into him and took a deep breath. He wondered how much pain and sorrow one person could take.

She shuddered and let out a deep cry. "He traded...himself... for me!" Her scream tore through the dusk.

Kent held her out from him, not letting her go, just holding her away to peer into her eyes. To reach her there. "I would expect nothing less from Jason, Wren. Right now, I've got to get you back, and then we'll find him. We'll find Jason."

She was shaking her head. Kent knew that was a bad sign.

"I'm not leaving him. I'm not going back."

Without even thinking about it, he flipped her over his shoulder. She pounded against his back and kicked and screamed as he made his way back to the truck with her and pushed her inside.

"Hold her. Do not let her go!" he said to Boyd.

Boyd looked terrified but did as Kent requested. It gave him just enough time to fill another syringe.

Over the cacophony Wren made, Marvin said, "Is that really the only answer you have? Just knock everyone out? That's your only solution to adversity?"

Kent was nodding his head rapidly. "If only I had a limitless supply," he said as he plunged the needle into Wren's upper arm. She glared at him as she fell asleep.

When the noise she made finally ceased, Marvin said, "That's the girl you wanted to rescue? I think my plan was better."

"Shut up," Kent said. "Hand me the radio, Boyd. And turn this thing around."

35

DAVIS

No sooner had they left than Davis realized how much pain he was in, and the fact that he was still barefoot. The wounds to his heels were freshly open, cracked and bleeding. Without the adrenaline rushing through his bloodstream, the pain came on full force.

The boy marched in front of him and slightly to the right as Davis kept the gun pointed relatively in his vicinity. He didn't expect him to pull anything...of course, that's when you should be worried. Except that the pain was distracting as hell.

"Slow down," Davis said. "I've gotta stop a second and grab my boots. You got anything in there to make a sling out of?"

Drone boy shook his head.

"Figures," Davis said and then looked up quickly as the boy began to tear away the lower hem of the shirt he wore.

"Hey, I didn't..." Davis began to say but then suddenly the young man held out the piece of fabric to him. "Thanks," he said. He was about to holster his handgun when he realized that was probably what the drone boy was waiting for to make his move. Davis could barely move his left arm with the increasing swelling.

"Nee tu…"

"No…don't try to talk. God…I know what I need to do. You stay right there and don't even attempt to move. Got me?"

The young man put his hands up in the air and nodded.

Davis saw his boots lying near the log he'd sat upon earlier… before the chasing and the shooting and kidnapping. *Oh, and the bleeding. Can't forget about the bleeding.* "Ask the universe and she shall deliver," Davis said as he flipped the med kit over. He knew the kid had no idea what he was referring to. It didn't matter to him. He sat down and looked at the kid for a long moment while he wiped off the blood on his shoulder and arm wounds with a balled-up, discarded shirt. Most of the bleeding had stopped. He opened the med kit. "Man, look what a difference a flood and a decade will make," he said as he stared into the pristine first aid kit's contents. "All those sanitary bandages." He located a few of the supplies he needed and sat the rest beside him. After that he used antibacterial ointment and bandages to seal the wounds for now.

Shaking his head, Davis couldn't believe drone boy even used his mouth to speak. These barbarians were relentless. And here he was, himself…one of them. He'd known of Hyde, fucking Hyde. Sick mother…that's what they all called him behind his back. His penchant for medieval torture devices was legendary. The man never had a friend in his life. No one could sleep at night around him. He was too freaking sick. Davis never had the displeasure of meeting him up close in person but saw him speak a few years ago in Astoria during a mandatory get-together. *Mandatory* was the code word used for be there or be dead. Even so, the guy had a way of creeping you out in an auditorium full of people. The difference between Hyde and the rest of criminal society was that he enjoyed it. He had no qualms about letting others know he enjoyed torture. It fascinated him.

Had Davis known then what was coming, a couple of stray

bullets to Hyde and Tale's heads would have meant justice and mercy to hundreds.

But then it's too late and now here we are.

At least Hyde was dead. And that's why he'd been sent to deal with them. He'd failed and now his family was likely going to die too if he didn't make it back soon. Having the kid with him, one of theirs, was all he could provide in exchange for his failures. They'd hurt him, might even kill him, but since he was a drone operator he certainly had more to offer than the girl. It might already be too late and if it was, Davis told himself, he'd do what he could to set the boy free before he killed Tale. That was his failsafe plan anyway. If he found out that his family was already extinguished...then all bets were off.

When Davis finished with his shoulder wounds, he sucked in a breath as he used a sanitary wipe to wipe away as much debris from his heels as possible and applied ointment to them as well. He added bandages only to keep road crap from sticking to the wounds, in hopes he'd receive real medical care in a few hours when they reached Astoria.

Slipping his modified boots back on, he said, "Right as rain," between gritted teeth. "Come on, Drone boy, let's go."

He didn't see fear in the kid's eyes, though. He patiently waited for him, even. It was like calling a dog to tag along on a walk. That was something curious about the situation. Anyone else would look for an escape. Tried to flee. Fumed at him... anything, but not this guy. Possibly it was because of the obvious torture. Maybe he was curious about Astoria. Hell, if he had it in for Tale with a plan for vengeance...he'd help the little bastard.

"What's your name, kid?"

The boy stopped walking, stared at him and raised an eyebrow.

"You can write it down. Don't try to talk. That's just creepy sounding. No offense."

Jason took out a ballpoint pen and ruffled paper pad, so worn the page edges curled up like wood shavings, from his zipped-up jacket pocket. It was getting colder. He scribbled something down in the center after using his palm to flatten a space between the curls and turned the pad over to show Davis.

"Jason. Nice name. I'm Davis. Sorry to make your acquaintance. Let's get going."

36

JASON

When Sloane had mentioned they needed a spy and he volunteered, he imagined there was a possibility of being recaptured. However, he didn't plan to stay captured. His goal was to find out where their camp was located and any valuable information along the way and he fully intended to do that, knowing he might be giving his life for the cause.

Having Wren safely away from this guy was a huge relief. Now if he could only get Davis to move along faster, they might make it before it was pitch dark. Visibility was an issue, but Davis's injuries were slowing him down.

Just when he thought he might just take his chances now and flee, Davis grabbed him by the scruff and pulled him forward as they walked around a bend in the road. "I know what you're thinking, kid. But you're not getting away."

That's when Jason saw the glowing fire lights up ahead. At first, he thought the entire bridge was on fire. That wasn't it. There were torches set up all along the way. As they came into the clearing, a Humvee barreled toward them.

Davis said close to the back of his ear, "I'm sorry, Jason. I didn't want to do this. You'll soon understand."

With the sun setting low across the water and the bridge lit up in torchlight, Jason was exposed. There was nowhere to run or try to escape.

As the Humvee came to a sudden stop in front of them, several men piled out. A lot of yelling ensued, though Jason could only see the angered faces of those surrounding him. Davis shoved Jason into the arms of two guards as a battered blue pickup showed up and a man stepped out.

"Hey," the guy said to Davis. They shook hands.

They talked for a few minutes while Jason stood there being frisked by the two guards. As they found the knife hidden in his jacket, Davis said, "Nice." And Jason smiled and shrugged one shoulder up.

The man talking to Davis reached for a handheld radio clipped on the side of his waistband. Jason's eyes lingered on the device for a few minutes as he spoke into it. This guy was white, tall, and lean with dark hair. He seemed familiar with Davis. Possibly a friend. And best of all, he had radio equipment.

The man pulled the radio away from his face and gave orders to the two guards holding Jason. One said something back to them and then Jason felt them pulling him away toward the Humvee.

Jason quickly scanned the blue pickup truck again, and the man holding the radio, before he was shoved in the back seat of the Humvee.

37

SLOANE

"What do you mean, you'll be here soon?"

Kent's voice bordered on hostile. She didn't blink. "I mean, we're on our way. You said Wren was shaken but looked otherwise okay?"

"Yes. Again...why are *you* coming *here*?"

"They have one of ours. They have Jason. We're ending this. We're ending this tonight."

"Sloane, stop." Kent's voice suddenly dropped. "I can't...I can't lose you. Look, come and pick up Wren and then go back. I'll take care of this. I'll get Jason back."

"No. We can discuss this soon. It's going to take more than you and me. We are going to fight back. We're going to win this."

She ended the call then and stared straight out the windshield at the littered road ahead.

"Well?"

She looked over at Chuck driving the Jeep.

"Wren's safe. She told Kent that Jason traded himself for her."

Chuck tightened his hands on the steering wheel and nodded. "I'd expect that of him."

"What will they do to him?"

He took a second to answer. "I um, I've only heard rumors but it's likely they won't let him live long. He's defective... though they made him that way. It doesn't matter. What he knows about us and his capability with the drones will give him some value, but any defeats or dependents detract from his worth."

"He doesn't have any dependents. They took him captive."

"I know. That's just the rules for their everyday citizens. He's a prisoner. God only knows what they'll do to him. Damn, I liked the kid."

"Don't refer to him as if he's dead. This is not over."

Headlights flashed out on the darkened road finally, letting them know they'd found them. Moments later, Sloane held her daughter in her arms, sitting in the laid-back front seat of their truck. Wanting to both scream at her and hug her at the same time, Sloane settled for just holding her groggy daughter.

"Mom? How did you get here?" Wren asked as she came to again. "Wait, where's Jason?" she asked, shaking, and struggled to sit up in the reclined seat. Then the horror flashed on her dirt-covered face. "Oh God."

"Wren...what can you tell us about the man who took him?" Sloane asked.

It was Kent who answered first. "We have all the information about this guy from Marvin. He's cooperating."

"Am not," Marvin said from the backseat.

Sloane looked around the seat at their prisoner. He couldn't make eye contact with her in his position, but he certainly was listening to their conversation.

"You're one syringe away from La-La Land, my friend. Keep it up."

Boyd, who was seated in the driver's seat still, stifled a laugh.

Sloane wasn't sure what was going on, but these guys had obviously been in the truck together for too long. She had a remedy for that.

As she motioned her head with a tilt, Kent followed her away from the rest to discuss their next move.

"Do you think you can get Marvin and his broken leg in the Jeep with us? I'd like to have Boyd take Wren home."

"We should all head home. Sloane, think about the possible losses."

"Do you think this is going to end if we don't bring it to them?" She shook her head. "No, I've been fighting them since Horseshoe Lane. I'm not doing this anymore. And I'm sure as hell not going to wait for them to come to our gates again. This ends now."

Kent held out his hand in a peace signal. "Okay, I just wanted to make sure."

"Kent, just have Boyd take Wren home now. We have to get going."

"I'm not going home!" Wren yelled.

Sloane looked around Kent to see her daughter standing nearby, with Boyd running to catch up with her.

"I'm sorry, she got up suddenly and ran after you guys before I could catch up," Boyd said.

"It's okay, Boyd. Wren, you need to listen. Boyd needs to take you back so that you two can take care of your sisters. They're alone without you."

Without a beat, Boyd stood there shaking his head, "I'm not going back without my sister. I'm sorry, Sloane. I can't do that. Someone else can take Wren back. It won't be me."

Everyone began to yell at once until Kent whistled.

Taking a deep breath, Sloane said, "You know we might not be alone out here. We have people watching but arguing in the dark near enemy territory isn't the best idea.

"Boyd, I understand what you're saying. I think you know the risks. That's your decision and I respect that.

"Wren, you're my daughter. You do as I say. You're going back because I need you to take care of your sisters and…"

"No, Mom. I'm not. I'm not going back and you can't make me."

"The fact is..."

"The fact is, I'm eighteen now. I can make my own decisions. I love and care about Jason. I'm as good a shot as any of you and I'm going. You need me. I can recognize the man who took him, too. You can't afford the resources it will take to send me back. Mae and Nicole are better off without me there."

Sloane's heart shattered in a way, right there. It wasn't because of her defiance...it was because she realized her daughter was right.

"You realize you could die or be captured and tortured. You realize this decision is irrevocable?"

"I already made that decision the moment I headed out to find Jason on my own. You should not have sent him...alone."

Sloane nodded. Her daughter was right on that one too, though that's what Jason wanted.

She swallowed and looked to the ground. "We're wasting time. Let's go."

38

DAVIS

They tossed the kid into the back of a van soon after their arrival. He was terrified. Not Jason...Davis. Why the kid had a knife on him and never tried to use it seemed odd but he figured Jason had his reasons.

Jason was stoic as hell. Davis didn't understand it. As they stole his backpack and remaining items from him and dragged him away, he only clipped his chin at him in a kind of acknowledgment that confused Davis.

It was Davis that was terrified. He was pretty sure he'd just handed Jason to his assassins, and he was about to find out the fate of his own family. He held this futile hope by a string that they were fine.

That's what they said when he climbed into the cab of the Humvee.

"Why'd you come back, man? You're late. You know what that means." Ivan always told it like it was.

"I'm aware. If you haven't noticed, I'm also alone and I'm beat to hell."

"What went down? God, you're a mess."

"I'll tell Tale once I'm assured of my family's welfare."

Ivan said nothing as he drove over the torch-lit bridge. His chiseled profile revealed nothing. The only signal was his clenched jaw as he stared straight ahead.

"You're not going to tell me? We go way back, man."

"You know I can't. Don't even."

He didn't give Davis a chance to ask more prying questions. He radioed ahead instead, even though Davis was pretty sure the doctor was already alerted that he was coming in.

"Get Doctor Keith up. Davis needs some TLC. She's going to need assistance."

Which meant to Davis that he had a long night of pain ahead of him. Doctor Keith was awesome. She was also very lucky to be the only doctor in town. Otherwise, her lesser gender superseded everything, despite her expertise. Davis even remembered a time they'd come across another doctor of the male variety. They could have brought him to Astoria. Ivan took one look at Davis and a silent decision passed between them. This guy wasn't coming with them. It would have meant her demise.

They protected one another in ways they never thought they'd have to, in little ways. Ways that mattered. It was a brutal way of life. As cutthroat as it came. Only once in a while they were able to preserve a little justice, though it always came at a price for someone else.

They came to a stop and Ivan put the vehicle in park.

"Look," Davis began to say.

"I can't help you. I wish I could."

It bothered Davis that Ivan said *you* and not *your family*. Maybe he was only imagining things. "I meant...like Dr. Keith... the boy, Jason's his name. He's like her. They're good people. They don't deserve this, but they can't protect themselves."

Grim-faced, Ivan just nodded.

It was the way he looked at him that made the dread overtake him. Ivan's hand was already on the door handle, ready to leave, but he said, "Did anyone make it? There's been a lot of executions lately."

Davis didn't expect the question. "I saw the bodies of all of them except for Marvin. He dropped down in a pit. I don't know if he made it or not. *Not* would be my guess."

"Just as well," Ivan said and stepped out of the cab, walking around to help Davis into the infirmary.

"I don't need your help," Davis said as Ivan took one arm.

"You do...you just don't know it yet," Ivan said as he helped him walk into the infirmary anyway.

It was as if his entire body suddenly realized he'd been shot twice, stabbed once and both of his feet were infected.

"What the hell happened to you?"

"Hi, Linda," Davis said.

Her hair. It was what made him smile, despite the circumstances, each time he saw her. It stood out like sunshine. The curliest mound of hair he'd ever seen on a white woman. Her personality matched. He almost always saw her with a smile. It depended on the company, of course. There were a few individuals in town you just didn't smile around.

Ivan helped him onto the table, waved goodbye and left.

The infirmary was located in a one-room house near Tale's office. He half-expected the guard to be there, but he was nowhere in sight.

Linda lived upstairs. Always, there was a guard standing outside on the wooden porch. It wasn't for her protection. She was not there of her own free will. None of them were, really. She didn't try to escape but she didn't make it easy for them to keep her there either. She'd been known to trick them a time or two. They'd finally gotten used to her ruses. Her only response was that they couldn't keep up with her. It wasn't her fault if they were lazy.

No longer were guards allowed to accept any kind of medication from her in trade for goods or looking the other way. She was too charming that way. And she had no dependents like the rest of them. She had no liabilities to be coerced with. That was the thing. The liabilities and the coercion. The advantage and the disadvantage. She held a little bit of power...a lot of good it did her. She was still held against her will.

"Take 'em all off."

"Geez, Linda," he said as he gingerly peeled his shirt away from his arm, then removed his boots as well.

Her eyebrows rose at the sight of the wounds on his heels. "Pants, too."

"Seriously? I don't have anything you need to see under there."

It was the way she smiled and tilted her head. "I'll be the judge of that. Besides, if you throw a clot or something while I have you under, I need quick access to your anus."

Shaking his head at her, he said, "That's just wrong, woman."

"It's not personal. Lie down, big guy," she said, holding a syringe over him.

"Don't," Davis said. "Don't put me to sleep."

She lowered her voice to something more tender. "You don't want me digging around in there with forceps while you're fully conscious, my friend. And I don't think you realize this, but I have to take a Brillo pad to your heels."

"Just do it, Linda. And tell me what the hell went on around here while I was on vacation."

She laid down the syringe on the metal table with a clank and picked up the forceps. As she shook her head, her wild curls bounced around, but she wasn't smiling. The sunshine was gone. "Nice try, but you know I can't do that."

The look in her eyes told him everything he needed to know, though. It wasn't good.

39

JASON

Jason could not hear the voices in the next room. They'd thrown him into a cinderblock cell and locked the door. There was nothing to sit on. Only a drain in the center of the cold concrete floor. The place looked very similar to another one, not too long ago. One he'd rather not remember. It was the drain that bothered him.

As of yet no one had tried to speak to him. They'd only taken his backpack and drone and patted him down, emptying his pockets and taking the knife he'd had hidden in there. The whole time, Jason remained calm, studying the faces and exits around him. One light remained on through the night. Jason, huddled in a corner, slid down the wall and finally fell asleep sometime later.

The next morning, he'd felt a vibration against the flooring that woke him. Opening his eyes, he saw a man standing at the gate with his mouth open. He didn't look too happy. Jason knew he must have slept through the initial greeting because now the man's lips were saying something he couldn't quite understand. The word *ass* was mentioned though, so Jason put it together that he wanted him to get up.

Jason stood against the back wall with his hands held up and out. The guard unlocked the gate and looked at him curiously, like he was some kind of moron, and then waved his hand for Jason to come through.

They were going to find out that he had less than stellar hearing soon. Who knew what would happen then.

Jason thought it didn't matter much. He expected the questioning, the torture. What did matter was that he'd accomplished part of his mission. He found out where they were. He was there. He'd yet to meet the big guy, though. The other part of his mission was to convey this information back to Cannon Beach.

He just needed to find a way to get that information to them. It wasn't going to be easy and he doubted he'd have an opportunity to escape. He knew that the moment he saw Davis's hands on Wren. Something changed in him. He'd committed then; even if the effort took his own life, he'd make sure these people never touched her again.

The guard walked Jason through an adjoining door to a room just as misery-clad as the last. He wasn't sure what these guys did with all their time, but decorating sure wasn't something they had a knack for.

There was a table, at least, in this one, with a few chairs and another guy who seemed to be looking at the guard behind him. Jason soon understood there was a conversation going on without his knowledge. You learn these things when your hearing is no longer useful. It was the intense gaze of the recipient of the conversation that clued you in. He was listening to something and about to respond. His dark shaved head, the intense black eyes, the glance quickly to Jason. Curiosity there.

Jason tried to turn around to see the moving lips of the first guard, but he nudged him the other way. Then the guy in front of him was drilling his black eyes into his. His mouth moved.

"You deaf?" were the words his mouth formed.

For a moment there, Jason wanted to smile and say, "Is that a rhetorical question?" But the guy's eyes...there was something tortured there, too. There was an unspoken recognition of one to another. In the end of the half-second debate with himself, Jason decided to simply nod. The truth was, he could hear some things...certain sounds but not others. Now was not the time to explain trivial distinctions.

The man pulled out a chair and motioned for him to sit.

Jason looked at the chair. Cracked his neck on both sides and turned in a stretch on each side of his waist.

"Getting ready, huh? Don't try anything, skinny man. You won't win."

Lithium by Nirvana began to play somewhere in the back of his mind. But the guy was watching him as he took his seat and Jason somehow turned down the tune within just a little bit. *Here comes the torture,* Jason thought. *First the mental, then the psychological, and finally the physical. They'll all come in their own time and intermingle and repeat, but I'm ready.*

The first guard said something to the second that caused him to nod in agreement, and then he left the room and closed the door.

Intense eye guy sat at the table before him. He took out a paper pad and pen but kept the items close to his side of the table.

Jason sat there and stared at him.

He looked as if he were trying to decide where to start. Then he looked sad, as if someone close to him had recently died. Perhaps it was one of the men they'd killed at their camp. If that was the case, Jason knew this meeting wasn't going to go well for him. The man finally looked up at him and said, "My name is Ivan. Do you understand what I'm saying?"

Jason nodded.

Ivan placed the pen on top of the paper pad and then slid the set over to him.

"Let's get started at the beginning. Who killed Hyde? That's the first question."

Jason nodded and diligently began scribbling on the pad. It took him a while to get all the lines straight, so he held the paper close and covered what he was writing. He wanted to be precise. When he finished, he slid the paper back over to Ivan, but he kept the pen poised for more, his eyebrows raised expectantly.

When Ivan looked up from the pad, his menacing eyes caught Jason's gaze first, then Ivan's fist swung over and grabbed Jason by the hair and landed his head hard down against the table top near the paper pad.

It was at just at the right angle that Jason could still see where he'd drawn the diagonal line through the x's on the grid.

Perhaps Ivan wasn't ready to play the game.

40

SLOANE

It wasn't until the first light of dawn that they'd hidden their vehicles around an old tire shop when they saw the glowing lanterns on the Young's Bay Bridge in the distance.

"There's no way they haven't spotted us yet," Chuck said.

"If they did, they don't care. Try to cross that bridge, then they care very much," Marvin said.

Sloane looked at the man so willing to give them information in the backseat. A sheen of sweat covered his face and neck. He was in pain and doing a damn good job of not showing it. "Kent, can you give him something more?"

Marvin immediately held up his hand. "No syringes. I don't trust you anymore."

Kent said something back, but Sloane wasn't paying attention then. She was looking at the bridge across the water. It was a long one.

Kent was trying to convince Marvin that he would give him just a little morphine this time, to take the edge off.

Marvin didn't believe him.

"Isn't there another bridge to the east of here?"

"Not any more. Tale took it down. Said it was too much of a

liability. He only kept this one because of the little airport on this side of the water," Marvin said.

"He has air capability?"

"He doesn't but occasionally there are visitors from Seattle. If he had air capability, you guys wouldn't exist."

"Why didn't he just send a ship, then? Defeat us by sea. He seems to have a lot of those."

Marvin shook his head. "No one questions him…it's one of his rules. But my guess would be that you guys are just a nuisance. He's in the business of supply and demand. Goods and services to major cities. He doesn't give a damn what happens beyond that bridge, unless of course, you get his attention. Which you did."

"By killing Hyde, you mean. By shutting down that operation?"

"Yes."

"Do you know what he was doing in that building of his?"

"I've heard the rumors. He was a friend of Tale's. But I think even Tale thought Hyde was creepy. So he sent him up out of the way to conduct his experiments and to glean supplies from the locals. There's always been a sadistic doctor associated with most dictators. Look at history."

"You think Tale's a dictator?"

"The worst kind you can imagine."

Sloane knew history. That statement sent goosebumps along her arms. "Okay. Can you tell me…are there any good people there? Anyone who would help us?"

Marvin nodded…the sweat on his brow increased. "There are good people in Astoria. But they won't help you. They've got too much to lose."

She gave Kent a silent nod then, and before Marvin knew it, Kent plunged yet another syringe into his skin.

Marvin cut his eyes over to Kent when he felt the needle prick his skin and said, "I swear, man…you have got a problem.

Payback's..." Marvin pointed to himself and then at Kent before he fell asleep, yet again.

"Is there something you can do to keep his pain level down without putting him to sleep? I need more information from him but I hate seeing him in pain like this," Sloane asked Kent.

He shook his head. "Not if I want to keep a reserve. Besides, I think I need to reset his leg. Something's not right in there."

Sloane nodded and stepped out of the truck and joined Chuck, her daughter, and the others in the next vehicle.

"Sloane, we've been talking...the problem with that bridge is the long jetty that leads up to the suspension bridge itself. It's wide open. They'll pick us off easily," Chuck said.

"And the other bridge is out of order. It's our only gateway," Sloane said.

"I can swim," Wren said.

Sloane nearly sucked in a startled breath. "We're not quite there yet, but yes, you're a great swimmer. It might come to that. We need to prepare. We have to move tonight, if it's not already too late to save him."

41

DAVIS

Davis wasn't proud of it but somewhere during Dr. Linda's pincushion experiment, he'd passed out. At least, that's what she'd told him the next morning. She was probably trying to conceal the fact that she'd slipped him a sedative, though. He wasn't sure. When she denied the accusation, he still had his doubts. Her poker face was legendary.

The thing that bothered him the most when he woke up wasn't that he was wearing only a thin gown to cover his manhood, but that he was also handcuffed to the bed.

"Is this for my own safety? Or for yours?" he said with a slightly veiled threat in his voice.

"I'm afraid not," she'd said.

"Thought not. When's he coming?"

"He arrived early this morning by plane, but you were asleep. He'll return around lunch, he said. Which is very soon, by the way."

His breathing quickened suddenly. "Linda," he said and jerked on the chain around his wrist. The metal clacked against the rail. "Tell me...I need to know."

"Shhh," she said and looked to the doorway. The guard. Her

guard…he was always out there somewhere, listening, and ready to betray her. "I can't."

"It makes a difference. If I have nothing to live for, I need to know."

She was shaking her head.

He didn't know what that meant. This was not the time for misunderstandings.

The footsteps…there were footsteps coming. "Linda!" he said in a hushed tone.

But it was too late when she edged closer to the bed.

"Good morning…sunshine."

It was him.

Linda straightened up and pretended to check the IV cords. She didn't make eye contact with Tale. She didn't even acknowledge that he'd entered the room. Instead, like a servant, she bowed her head and exited, just after she winked one eye at Davis.

She'd given him hope in the smallest of movements. She'd given him everything, right there.

42

JASON

By the time the other guard came back to bring, or rather carry, Jason to his cell, his nose was offset from its normal position. This had happened before. Jason was pretty sure it was broken again. The blood continued to stream down his shirt. He tried to hold his head up to stem the tide. His left eye was also swelling shut, which made him dizzy when he tried to walk. He doubted he'd be able to see out of his eye by morning. In all, he thought Ivan held back a little. He'd expected more of him. Something wasn't right there. Toward the end, Ivan held him up by the shirt to steady him more than to punch him. His eyes betrayed him, from what Jason could see. Finally, the difference came to him.

Ivan didn't like the torture. He was only doing the job because he had to. They were watching him. Despite that, he was making a good show of things. There was no permanent damage…unless you counted the broken nose. But by this time, Jason just added this to his collection of injuries. He briefly wondered if his sense of smell would also be taken from him along with his hearing and taste. Jeez, that just left feeling and sight.

Strewn paper from the pad littered the floor of the gloomy

room when they took him away. One of them had a hangman game, penned in haste and blood-smeared. The lines were crooked for the last two letter spaces. He tried to make them perfect. But Ivan had caught on to his shenanigans in the last seconds and tore his artwork away from him, to land where it now lay on the floor.

Ivan handed Jason over. The guard held Jason up now, steadying him in a standing position. It was getting harder to breathe. He was facing the guard and away from Ivan. They were having a conversation. When Jason glanced at the guard's face, he mouthed the words, "They don't call you Ivan the Adopter for nothing."

Or something like that. The guy had a beard so it wasn't easy to tell what he was saying. Maybe it was Ivan the Clopper? That would make more sense. Ivan the Clobber-er? Hell, maybe it was Chopper. That would be bad. Ivan the Dropper? This whole lip-reading thing wasn't a perfect science and his eyes were getting blurry anyway.

He never did really figure it out since the guard was now hustling him to the cell again, shoved him inside and slammed and locked the door with a clang. Jason turned suddenly. He'd heard the clang. There was something about that high-pitched metal strike.

The guard looked at him and tilted his head.

Jason diverted his gaze from the gate to the floor. He shuffled over to the corner of the cell and slid down, tilting his head up in the corner in hopes the bleeding would stop. The last thing he wanted to see was his own blood trailing a river to the drain again. That was his new goal in life. Never let his blood go to waste.

43

SLOANE

Sloane walked through the night, oblivious to the light rain soaking her hair.

"Thankfully, it's a new moon tonight," Chuck said as he strapped on the heavy backpack. "The only light we have to deal with is the reflection of the torches along the bridge."

"Be careful with that thing. Don't drop it," Kent warned.

"Yeah, that would be bad," Chuck said.

Sloane almost smiled at the guy's banter. She was too busy thinking of all the truly bad things that might happen soon.

Her daughter caught her look. She wasn't smiling at all. She was dead serious as she zipped up her hoodie.

"Are you sure you can swim with that thing if you need to?" Kent asked her.

Wren nodded. "I've done it before."

"That's when the water wasn't near freezing and waving at you. This is different," Chuck warned.

"I know what it is," Wren said defiantly.

"No. You don't, sweetheart. That water will suck your breath away stone cold and freeze your limbs as soon as you plunge into it. There's a big difference here, kid. I know you think you're tough but you're not that tough," Chuck said.

Wren glanced at her mother in a plea for intervention.

Sloane said nothing. Her daughter needed to hear it.

"Swimming in the ocean off the beach is one thing. Getting slammed against the jetty rocks will take more than your breath away. You have to be realistic, Wren. You go down, then I have to deal with your mom and dad in basket case mode. That's going to ruin this whole vacation we're on. Do you understand the risks?" Chuck said.

Her daughter was probably pale as a sheet, but Sloane couldn't tell in the darkness. She did see that Wren had nodded her head.

"Okay, then," Chuck said and walked away.

Sloane let the lecture sink in a second and then said, "He's right, Wren."

"I know, Mom."

But that was all Sloane would say. Her daughter walked off with the crunch of gravel beneath her boots. Sloane regarded the little group there. She knew she shouldn't think it, lest she manifest the future, but she couldn't help knowing they'd return with fewer of them. They were prepared as much as possible and sitting on the ends of truck beds after readying their gear. Most of them were in quiet thought. She clapped her hands to get their attention, "Let's get moving. We need the cover of dark to pull this off, and it's wasting."

She leaned into Kent as the others began to walk away.

He drew her into him, his smell forever something she could not live without. His hand reflexively found the skin on the small of her back and inched south. As he whispered in her ear, "I can't believe I'm letting you do this," his brow furrowed.

"You never had a choice," she said with a smile.

He swallowed and then nodded, hugging her, perhaps for the last time. "Return to me," he said.

"Haven't I always?"

She didn't let him answer the question. She ran after the others to catch up. Kent would stay with Marvin and check in with their radios.

She saw their silhouettes in the distance against the glow of the firelight, specifically the outline of her daughter. Boyd's was hard to miss as he kept close to Wren, still feeling the need to pay his guilt debt to her. She knew this trip wasn't going to help that cause. His little sister was more than likely gone by now. These people held no life sacred, it seemed. Not even a child's. But there was no way she could keep Boyd from trying to find her.

More than anything, she wanted to banish these people from the Cannon Beach area. Sloane had no qualms about killing those of them willing to do harm to innocent lives. Then again, she also knew a few might die with what she was about to do. Was she any better than her enemy? She couldn't think about that right now.

Finding Jason and shutting them down was her mission at the moment. Soul-searching would have to wait another day or two.

By the time they'd rounded the final building, the torchlights illuminating the center bridge were in full view. It looked like something out of a medieval romance movie, only there should be a castle and a prince on the other side. Not a damn psychopath.

"Mom," Wren said in a hushed whisper. "Come on," she urged with a tilt of her head as she held the boat steady over the rocky shore.

Sloane stepped in and then Wren came in behind her, pushing off with her foot. Boyd nudged them farther over a low coming wave. There were three boats.

Was anyone watching them?

All heads were on a swivel approaching the open shoreline near the jetty. Those they assumed kept watch of the bridge either didn't want to approach them and kept to themselves or they'd vanished, sensing that trouble would soon come too close to them.

She and the others rode wave after wave and kept clear of the rocky shore. Paddling was difficult and more than once she sensed Chuck wanted to curse out loud.

The roar of the waves pretty much kept them from speaking, though they'd avoided that anyway. Words traveled faster over water.

Before they'd left, Sloane had looked out over the waves and realized the torchlight actually played to their advantage.

"We have to stick to the shadows before we can approach the center suspension bridge. The flames actually dilate their vision, instead of illuminating the waters below. Their focus has always been to light up the bridge, which means they can't really see much out over the water. It's our only advantage."

Chuck and the others agreed. The next part of their plan was less advantageous.

44

DAVIS

Davis stared at the ceiling, chewing on the inside of his left cheek. They'd handcuffed him for a reason. He could never stand the sight of Tale. The cuffs were for that man's safety, not his own. But if there was a glimmer of hope...he had to wait for the right opportunity.

"He's back from the wasteland," Tale said, placing one hand on the metal bedrail.

Davis glanced at it. There was a gold ring upon his tattooed finger. He wanted to break the damn thing off and shove it down the man's throat. How many times did he witness this monster kill the innocent? Did he do this same atrocity to his own family? As far as he knew, he only kept a few whores, but they didn't last long. That's why he didn't want to take the girl with him. He didn't want to have that responsibility weighing on his conscience as well as every horrible thing he'd done in the past to appease this monster.

Could Tale have killed his wife and boys and stand before him like this?

Yes. Only Tale was that demented.

He didn't carry the same human quality inherent in even the

worst of criminals. He had no sense of guilt, shame...nothing like that. Not even a glimmer. An empty soul, and that had to end soon. Now more than ever, Davis realized he should have sacrificed himself long ago to rid the earth of this man. He'd been a coward. He'd lived in fear. Just like all the others under his control...he'd failed humanity. But not for long. Tale's days were numbered. That was a promise he made then and there.

"Why are you here, Davis?" Tale said with a slight lilt of sarcasm in his voice. It was a rhetorical question. "Did you come back to warn me of some possible danger? I asked myself this question when I heard of your return. I send you guys out with clear instructions. You know the consequences. You had a job to do. You failed. So why'd you return?"

Davis seethed. Perhaps Linda was wrong. Perhaps it was foolish to hope.

"Oh," Tale chuckled. "I see. You brought back one of theirs. You think that's enough to make up for your failures? He's just a kid, and I hear he's useless to me anyway. So he knows how to fly a couple of gadgets. What the hell is that? And apparently Hyde already spent some time with him. He's just a liability to me now. I have no use for him or the people he came from. That's why I sent you to do your job."

Davis swallowed but still said nothing. His hands were balled into fists as he tried to twist them through the openings of the cuffs.

Tale clicked his tongue three times, as if he were chastising a child.

"Oh, you thought I'd spare your dependents...that's what you thought. There was a reckoning, Davis. You knew there would be."

His fist jerked up, pulling the chain taut suddenly.

Tale smiled.

With dead eyes, Davis drilled into his stare.

Two guards appeared behind Tale. Beyond them, Linda stood

in the doorway, shaking her head. Was she was denying what Tale said? Or giving him false hope?

Davis didn't know what to believe beyond the fact that it didn't matter now. Tale was as good as dead. This man would end soon.

"The question remains, what do I do with you now? No one is allowed to stay *without* dependents. Not even you, Davis. Linda? Are you done with him?"

She walked forward. She still did not look him the eye. "He's in no condition to leave here. He needs a few more days. He can't even walk."

Tale stared at him and seemed to think about his options for a while. Then finally, with a tilt of his chin, the guards went ahead and removed the cuffs, tightening them instead behind him. "Take him to the hold," Tale said.

Davis knew the guards. Knew there was no talking to them. Bribery wouldn't work, either. They were too scared, with too much to lose, just like he was—or had been.

"You can't do that. He's..." but that was all Linda said before Tale landed a hard strike across her face.

She fell to the side and landed on the ground with a thud.

"Don't ever tell me what I can or can't do!" Tale roared.

Everyone stopped. Even the guards.

Tale stormed out, eating the ground as he did.

"Someone...someone help her up," Davis said.

But the guards paid no attention to his words and instead began to haul him away, one on either side. It was true, Davis was in no condition to be out of that bed, but still he struggled with them. "Dammit, make sure she's okay. Don't leave her like this," he said as they took him from the room.

She hadn't moved from where she'd landed on the concrete floor. Her wild curls covered her face.

45

JASON

The damp cold made Jason shudder with chills. He wrapped his arms around himself tighter and huddled closer to the corner wall. Occasionally someone would come in, it seemed at regular intervals. He was making mental notes. If they wanted his attention, they threw wads of paper at him, which Jason collected and stuffed inside his jacket for more insulation. Never let a good thing go to waste.

So far, no one had brought him anything to eat though, let alone water to drink. That told him a thing or two. He wasn't likely to remain a guest for long.

Then something made him jerk up. It was that sound again. The metal strike. When he looked up, two men were dragging a third man inside the cell next to his. There were only two cells in the small holding room, jail or whatever you wanted to call it. This guy was in a hospital gown, though. They hadn't even bothered to give him underwear. His bare ass hung out for all to see. *Poor schmuck...wait a minute. That's Davis.*

Not that he'd seen his butt before, but he could tell from behind that it was him...it was the bandaged heels that gave it away.

They let him go and Davis caught himself from falling by leaning against the back stone wall. He said something to them as they left. It was probably not a kind word, Jason assumed. Then the door closed.

Jason couldn't help but stare at him. The man held sorrow too visible on his shoulders. It seemed his plan had failed if he'd landed himself in here.

Davis turned then, and his eyes met Jason's. Jason nodded as if to say, *Hi bro*.

Davis returned the gesture, then walked to the adjoining bars.

"Get up," he said.

Jason wasn't sure what he wanted.

"Get up. Get off the floor," he said again, but this time his face looked a little angry.

Jason shook his head. Heck, it was cold.

Davis pounded hard on the railing. "Get up, you little bastard. You're going to get hypothermic like that. Get up! Move around," Davis said, gritting his teeth.

What the...? Jason thought. *You don't get to tell me what to do. Why the hell do you care?* But Jason found himself sliding up from his seated position anyway. When he did, several of the pieces of paper dropped from the stuffing beneath his jacket.

Davis looked at the paper on the ground and shook his head. "You...need to move around. Build your body heat. Do some fucking jumping jacks."

Jason shook his head. *I'm not doing any fucking jumping jacks.*

"Do them," Davis yelled.

Jason shook his head again and took a step back.

Davis hit the railing again. He looked so pissed he might even turn into the Hulk at any second.

Dang...what the hell's this guy's problem?

"You wanna see your little girlfriend again? Do what I say. Do ten jumping jacks. You're fucking shaking."

Jason understood then...but he shot him the bird anyway and

then, instead of doing jumping jacks, he landed himself on the floor, pushed up, jumped up and repeated the burpees to the count of ten. His limbs were numb with cold but with each one, feeling returned.

When he was finished, he saw that the guard had come into the room again. He was handing Davis a blanket through the railing.

Why didn't they give him a blanket? Jason wondered. Those guards played favorites.

But then again, Davis's ass was bare...so there was that. No one wanted to see that.

This wasn't just any guard, though. It was Ivan...the chopper or whatever. While they were talking, Davis pointed to Jason and said something he couldn't quite make out with his head turned to the side.

Ivan shook his head. It was probably over the blanket. Maybe Davis asked him to give him one too? That would be nice of him.

Ivan turned to leave, and Davis asked him something else, but Ivan's jaw clenched, and he never looked back as he left the room.

Jason looked to Davis then. The man stared at the floor, clenching his blanket in his hands, then looked up at him. His eyes met Jason's. Something horrible had happened to him but he didn't think he'd want to talk about it. Get it off his chest. Nothing like that. This guy wasn't touchy feely. Davis's look changed then, as if he'd made a decision. He stared at Jason and mouthed, "Ten more."

46

SLOANE

"First of all, I don't recommend this. You're all going to die horrible deaths, but I know you won't listen to me. When you get there, to the other side, you'll have to avoid going ashore along the main road. There's a nice old Bayfront Best Western to the left," Marvin had said.

She nodded, thinking perhaps she'd seen it once a long time ago, when things were normal. That seemed a lifetime ago now.

"Don't go there. That's where a lot of the guards live. Instead, take the boats to the right under the bridge. Follow along the shoreline until you see a couple of buildings. One was a coffee shop but was demolished in the wave. There's a house after that, and a rusted old building that's barely standing up. One more place down is a blue or purple auto parts store. I can't remember which. You can't miss it. No one will be there. It was looted a long time ago of anything useful. The doors are open. Start there. You guys can regroup and catch your breath. Then you can cross the street into the greenbelt that runs west through this neighborhood," he said as he drew the map. "You'll have to skip through a couple of streets. Most of these people aren't going to give a crap what you're doing but every now and then, some jackass will squeal on you just for brownie points. So don't get caught. That'll take you to the road you came in on. Then...if you made it that far, which I doubt," Marvin glanced at her then, "you should see the blue and teal building with an orange roof, the Port of Astoria Building, down Portway Street from there." He shook his head as if trying to figure out the best way to proceed. "If I were you, I'd pick my way across. It's hard to tell until you get there, but you're pretty much out in the open. Take cover behind the various buildings. Or you could head to the marina and skirt along the edge, maybe go up the Riverwalk. You'll have to use your best judgment.

"Tale...he'll be there if he's in town. And by now, I'm pretty sure he's going to be there. That's where Davis will be, and the boy you're looking for. More than likely, they put Davis in the hold with the boy."

"Why would they do that?" Sloane asked.

For a minute there she thought Marvin was going to cry. The grown man's eyes teared up, but he took a deep breath and said, "Because he's now a danger to Tale. You don't understand. In Astoria, if you don't return on time or disappoint him in any way, he takes away your dependents."

"Takes them away?"

"He kills them. He calls it a reckoning. That's what I've been trying to tell you. You can't live there without dependents and if you mess up, your dependents cannot live without you. Do you understand now? You understand why I know there's no reason for me to return? My family...my wife and two boys. They're gone."

"So you think Davis returned anyway with Jason in hopes his family was still alive?"

Marvin nodded. "I think he's hopeful but...there's no way. It's happened too many times. I've seen it happen too many times. If Davis returned, they have him in lockup to keep him from threatening Tale. That's if they haven't already killed him."

"If we discover Davis in there, what should we do with him?"

Marvin thought about that scenario for a second. "Open the door quickly and run like hell. Get out of his way. If you don't take Tale down, he will."

"Are there any friendlies we can depend on in case we get caught up?"

Marvin shook his head again.

She could see he was holding back the physical pain as much as he could at that point but his words were important.

"There is one. Her name is Linda. She's the doctor but if you end up in her care you're screwed anyway. She's the only one without dependents and only allowed to live because she's so useful. Tale keeps her under constant surveillance, though."

"Okay," she said. This man had helped them more than he knew. She couldn't thank him enough but that would wait. She had to complete the job first. She got up to leave when he grabbed her arm.

"Wait. Listen, if you get him, you can't leave there without blocking that damn bridge. That's why we're all in this mess."

"The Young's Bay Bridge? We'll do what we can on our way out."

"No," he shook his head, "no, the big one. Over the Columbia River, the Astoria-Megler Bridge."

"Wait. That's a huge bridge. It's what connects Oregon to Washington State over the Columbia." Now she was the one shaking her head. Blowing up a smaller bridge to secure them regionally over Young's Bay was hard enough. Destroying the big bridge over the Columbia would mean cutting them off geographically north. Sure, they could get around to the east if they had to, but far out of their way. Suddenly, she realized she was making decisions for the next few generations. That was a lot of pressure. Without modern equipment, there was no replacing that thing. "Why do you think that bridge brought all of this on?"

"Because one tyrant meets another and the next thing you

know we have wars and crap. The fewer numbers we have, the more likely you weed out the psychopaths before they get to power. If you block that bridge somehow, we buy ourselves a little bit of peace and quiet on this side, at least for a time. You can deal with nuts in a vacuum, you just crush them. It's the ones you can't see coming...those are the ones you worry about."

She understood now, and she had more questions for him, especially about the airfield, but Kent was ready at that point with another injection. Marvin was done for now. His advice might have just saved them all.

She was now on the boat trying to remember all of Marvin's words, everything he tried to impart to her, when they reached the center suspension on the pylons of the Young's Bay Bridge. It had taken long enough, and they were only halfway there. The wind was so sharp it stole your breath away. One of the three boats stayed behind, the one with Chuck and his backpack. He had something to do there first, and it would take a while.

She waved her hand at him as they continued on with the other two boats. First slipping under the bridge to the edge of the other side, with her head peeking up, she looked for anyone scanning the horizon and waited. After a time, no one showed themselves, which led her to believe her assumptions were true. They were only concerned with the bridge itself. Soon, that wouldn't be an issue for them if she had her way.

47

DAVIS

The kid was sweating now. He'd even taken off his jacket. When Davis was first brought into the holding cell, he was trembling and his lips were the wrong shade of blue. He'd seen it happen in here before and hell, he'd practically handed the kid to these morons. He felt responsible for him.

He'd hoped his old friend Ivan would help him, but something had changed in the man since he'd last seen him. Before, they'd plot and steal little victories but now something was off. Something had happened while he was gone, and Davis had no idea what that was. Maybe he had to witness the death of Davis's family. That was probably what it was. It scared him, too. Though Davis realized his boys and wife were probably dead now, he wanted revenge and Ivan only had one dependent, a teenage nephew that was training as a guard. Heck, he'd moved out into the soldier's barracks and taken a wife of his own already. That left Ivan with no dependents and vulnerable to Tale's whims. He wasn't sure how Tale reconciled that situation with his rules. That left Ivan open, with nothing to lose. But when Davis tried to talk to him about it earlier, he said nothing and left.

"Are you done?" Davis asked Jason.

The boy nodded.

"Put your jacket back on. Keep your body heat inside. You're going to need it."

The kid looked at him like he was crazy.

"Now."

Jason reluctantly slipped his jacket back on and zipped it up. That was when Ivan returned with another blanket in hand and a couple of bottles of water.

"That's generous of you, but how 'bout some pants?" Davis said.

"Just don't tell anyone where you got these."

"You can do better than that, Ivan. What the hell's going on here? I need to know. Just tell me if I have something worth fighting for."

Ivan didn't make eye contact nor answer the question but instead slipped the blanket between the cell bars. Davis grabbed Ivan's forearm holding the blanket. "What happened to my family, Ivan? Tell me!"

Ivan jerked back from his hold and still...his eyes would not meet Davis's.

"Trust me when I say get the hell out of here. Leave, Davis. That's the only thing I can say. You have no dependents now."

That's when Ivan raised his eyes to meet his. There was not just pain but deep sorrow there.

Davis wasn't sure what to make of it. He released his friend's arm. He let him go and took the blanket and the two bottles without another word.

Ivan stopped near the door, turned and nodded to Davis. It was one of those last looks you give a good friend. A kind of farewell.

After the door shut, Davis found the ridged knife wrapped in the blanket. He didn't show the kid. Instead, he handed the other blanket to Jason and also handed him one of the water bottles. The boy had to be thirsty.

Davis turned his back on the boy and opened the blanket, studying the knife. Something shook in the hilt. There was a screw cap. When he opened it, he found a lighter loose inside the cavity. Before he could think what the heck Ivan was up to, he had to turn abruptly because the kid behind him was spewing and choking on something.

When he looked, the kid stared at the water bottle in his hands as if the clear liquid contents were poison.

Davis opened his own bottle and smelled...nothing. He took a taste and then realized what Ivan had done. Vodka.

48
IVAN

So much screaming. He couldn't tell who was more hysterical. The mothers, of course, but there were a few of them. All terrified.

"You have to decide, Ivan. Which one will it be?"

If only he could kill the man and get away with it.

"Sir, please, with all due respect, I can take them all." His voice had a quiver in it when he spoke. He had to avoid looking weak, desperate.

Tale shook his head and laughed. "You already have one recent dependent. I can't let you take them all. There are consequences for the actions of your friend. What kind of precedent does that set for the others? I won't spare them just for you. I was already lenient with one of the abandoned families. I'll let you choose *one* of these. That's it. One of the boys or the wife? Which one will it be? Tell me now, Ivan. *Now*, Ivan!"

"I can't," he said, looking at them all. "I can't choose."

"Then they all die," Tale said with a slide of his chin.

Ivan ran forward as the rifles raised. He grabbed one of them, jerked the boy from his mother's side, just as the rifles began to fire.

It was a moment he'd never forget. The boy's mother looked at him in that last surreal moment. Both hatred and humanity at once. She'd died in the next second but her slow motion end told him everything. He'd grabbed the boy as the kid tried to run back to his mother despite the gun blasts. Held him forcibly against his chest, keeping him from turning to look at the horror unfolding.

Later that day, Linda looked the boy over. He wasn't talking. He was in shock. There was no doubt he'd seen and heard too much, despite Ivan's efforts. Like a limp doll, Ivan slung the boy over his arm and carried him home. Inside the door, the girl had already prepared dinner. She was only seven or eight and already doing a grown woman's work. He landed the boy on the floor as if saying to himself, *Here's another to add to my collection.*

Everyone else thought Ivan's motives were insurance. A way to stay alive. That wasn't it at all. Before the girl came to him, his only thought was to get rid of Tale. Now, these two children were his weakness. Ivan the Adopter. That's what they called him now.

49

SLOANE

It was Sloane's own hand that cast them afloat out from beneath the safety of the bridge, with anything but a devil-may-care attitude. Anyone really looking over the side into the water would see them without a doubt. As the two boats continued to fight the waves, Sloane faced the other way, leaning back with her rifle aimed and ready. Surveilling the bridge activity through her scope, her pulse quickened when she noticed a few guards walking along the bridge. One was running and for a second, she thought perhaps he'd noticed Chuck below the bridge, but after a few moments she realized he was just jogging along the perimeter. There was no haste in his steps, just a steady rhythm. These people were doing a job, she realized. There was no heart in their efforts. They were merely running the clock to their shift, unlike the people of Cannon Beach, who took things a little more seriously. Guard watch meant something to her people. Life and death.

Wren raised her hand suddenly, and in the inky black of night, she'd only noticed because her arm blocked the torchlight of the bridge. She pointed to the approaching land. Sloane turned and saw they were getting closer, but it was so dark, she could not tell one building from the next, let alone between one that was blue or purple. Again, Wren silently led them to the right. The youthful eyes on her daughter came in handy.

Without a word, the two boats ran the rocky shore. Someone from each vessel jumped out into the breach between water and land and pulled them in. They tried their best to mute the sounds of the metal scraping on the rocks beneath but with the waves creating their own cacophony, she didn't think it really made much difference unless someone had a trained ear for detecting a different cadence to the waves' rhythm. Still, they could not be too careful. It would only take one person to blow their cover. Sloane stepped out of the boat as the others completed their tasks. She aimed again at the bridge, looking for Chuck through the scope. The third boat was coming their way. She tried waving an arm to show their location, but they didn't indicate they'd seen her yet.

"Mom, they're off course," Wren whispered close by.

"Let them get closer. They'll spot us."

It wasn't as if she could set off a flare highlighting their location. "Come on, come on..." she murmured under her breath when they looked as if they were going to veer farther up shore, and then someone in the boat finally raised their hand against the backdrop of the flames on the bridge and they course-corrected toward them at last.

"Whew, the last thing we need is to lose one another now."

As the boat neared, Chuck jumped out and pulled the others ashore. He and the others efficiently picked up the third boat as Sloane kept watch when suddenly, someone lost their hold on one end of the boat, sending the metal edge crashing hard against the side of a slate boulder.

"What was that?"

The unknown voice made them crouch on the gravel beach in the dark.

Sloane aimed at the person above them but shooting off a

round now would blow their cover. They were exposed there in the dark. The man above them looked directly over their position, his eyes fixed on the bridge instead of below. Had there been moonlight, their deaths would have been eminent.

Sloane didn't dare breathe as the man muttered, "Screwing off as usual."

He sounded older, disgruntled even. He turned to leave but then he turned back again as someone in her group must have slipped a foot in the gravel.

"Someone there?" the raspy voice said.

A beam of light suddenly blinded Sloane.

Her finger on the trigger, she began to pull when suddenly there was a hard thunk and the man let out a moan. The beam of light disappeared into the tall grasses above the shore.

Scurrying sounds in the gravel. She too ran toward where the man had been.

"Good job, Wren," Chuck whispered.

Someone doused the flashlight but before then, Sloane watched in the light of the beam as Wren pulled the arrow from the man's neck. Her daughter had just saved them all.

Sloane turned again and watched the bridge guards. Their heads bobbed along the edge. They seemed not to notice their tiny invasion at all.

50

JASON

This, he realized, was the reason he didn't drink. How in the world did people consume this stuff? His entire throat burned like hell and he couldn't stop coughing. Worse yet, he had no actual water to rinse his mouth with.

The liquid in the bottle didn't smell like alcohol, but it certainly tasted like it. What a crappy trick. *Ivan's a jerk*, Jason thought as he tried to catch his breath. Heaving air in felt as if he were breathing in flames. He looked up and saw that Davis was practically yelling at him and raised his finger to his mouth, shushing him angrily. Jason tried to read his lips but realized it didn't matter. A string of curse words would not help his predicament.

Jason was about to pour the liquid in the bottle down the drain in the middle of the floor when Davis went absolutely bat-shit crazy and lunged his arm between the bars, reaching for the bottle in Jason's hand. That's when the blanket he held fell harder to the floor than it should have on its own, exposing a big knife.

Then...then the door of the jail began to open, sending Davis to fling the edge of the blanket over the knife with his bare foot.

The other guard, not Ivan, the one with the beard, said something like "What's going on in here?"

Davis's head was turned away. He seemed to be reasoning with the guy.

Suddenly Jason understood. He took the bottle again, as if it wasn't the worst thing he'd ever tasted, and took a swig, all nonchalant like, and screwed the cap back on. The guard glanced in his direction. Davis pointed at him. Jason bobbed his head up and down as if to agree with whatever Davis was saying. Like, "Yep, nothing to see here. He just choked on the, uh...water. What an idiot." Or something like that, Jason imagined. Meanwhile, the inside of Jason's mouth felt like it was burning away the lining.

The guard left and when Jason looked at Davis, he was sweating, even though he was still only dressed in a nightgown without an ass covering.

Jason lifted his arms and opened his mouth, like, *What's going on?*

"What do you mean, what the hell? You nearly blew it."

Jason pointed at himself, and shook his head, no, and pointed at Davis again.

Davis walked over to the bars separating them and said, "It doesn't matter now, kid. Look, you need to make a decision here. Right now. I'm leaving. You have two choices. You can either come with me and get killed or, you can stay here and get killed. What's it gonna be?"

"Fuh," Jason said, shaking his head.

51

SLOANE

Roll call. Sloane quickly counted them as they entered the cleared building.

Wren said, "I thought Marvin said the building was blue or purple, it looks more periwinkle. Am I right?"

No one answered the question.

"We've got it. We're all here," Sloane said with relief. "Now a hike through the woods. Wren, no jabbering unless necessary. Chuck, you're taking up the rear. Everyone else in between. If you need to adjust your gear, take a restroom break or heck, if you need to pray, do it now. We leave in two minutes."

"Yes, Mom," Chuck said. "I can't remember the last time someone asked me if I needed a potty break. I feel like a two-year-old."

"You'll thank me later," she said with a smile. "Let me remind all of you...keep the chatter down unless necessary. This is their turf, not ours."

Heads nodded. She knew they were getting nervous. She could feel the anxiety rising in her gut as well. They could be found out at any moment, attacked and killed, their little invasion done for.

Two minutes later, they spied out the front side entrance to the building. Except for the occasional fire from a torch or lantern, there were no signs of life from the homes across the street. Sloane did something then that she instantly regretted. She thought she could treat her daughter as one of the others but the moment she led the first group across the empty expanse, leaving Wren to come with the second group, her anxiety level skyrocketed. She couldn't think about everyone's safety, just hers. This was the danger. She wasn't built for that when her daughter was present among them. *Plan B,* she thought.

As soon as the second group made it clear to the edge of the evergreen buffer, she switched Boyd for Wren. "Nothing personal, I just can't function properly when I know she's that far away."

Boyd lifted his hands. "None taken."

"God, Mom," Wren said.

"Argue with me later," Sloane said. "No time now."

Their first journey by foot brought them out into the open, across a two-lane road, into a parking lot and then the evergreen buffer behind it. They followed that concealment northeast and then ran through a couple of backyards until they reached Florence Ave. Again, through a couple of backyards to Alameda Avenue and then they entered the evergreens again.

As they stopped to catch their breath, Wren said, "Why aren't there any dogs barking around the neighborhood? That seems odd to me."

"They ate them," Chuck said. "More than likely," he added with a lift of his shoulder. Sloane didn't doubt his words but gave him the stink-eye anyway, followed by, "Shh."

As they kept watch and caught their breaths, Chuck said, "You know, instead of risking the backyards, we could just skirt the street the rest of the way. The coverage from here on out seems minimal anyway."

She nodded. "I was considering the same path. We just have to get to Portway. Just a couple of blocks away. Does it seem too easy to you too? That's the feeling I'm getting. No dogs. No lookouts."

He took in a slow breath, then shook his head. "I think this is the way it is here. Those inside the walls live at the whim of a tyrant. People will only take that so long. It's been a while. Perhaps those that challenged him are dead and the rest are content living in the shadows. Or else they're too damn complacent, just like the guards on the bridge. Their focus is outward, not inward."

"That's deep, Chuck." But really, he was right. Or at least, she hoped so. "Well, let's get rid of the menace," she said, and they trekked their way through the night along Almeda Avenue up to the point through the woods where the Oregon Coast Highway met at a tee with Portway Street.

This was the area Marvin warned them about. How to proceed? Go from open parking lot, building to building, or make their way to the Riverwalk's edge and skirt along the shadows of the riverbank?

As she looked out, many of the buildings were destroyed from the carnage of the past. Most of them were collapsed in one area or another. Old rusted-out vehicles crowded the Oregon Coast Highway. She found it odd. As a leader of a community, she would have rid the town of things like this long ago, making a point of pride in their living conditions again. But Tale was not out to impress or take care of his people. It was all for him.

"What is that smell?" Wren whispered, and Sloane wanted to clock her for making any kind of noise at the moment.

But it *was* a remarkable odor. The stench could only be described as rotting, infected sewage...if that had a smell and she was sure it did, and it was festering inside her nose at the moment. In all likelihood it was a fish market gone way bad. This was a smell your nose did not get used to with extended exposure. How could these people live here?

Though at the moment she was looking for the three-story

orange rooftop Marvin described earlier, and down Portway Street at 1 Pier Street, she spied the building only because someone had erected what looked like a bonfire in the nearby parking lot. The flames highlighted the front of the building.

At second glance, the fire had to be a makeshift lighthouse, signal fire. The silhouette of two people with rifles slung over their shoulders indicated it was probably an around-the-clock guard detail. That's where Tale had to be located, and Jason as well. That was also a good indication the building was secure and guarded. She hoped they were as lax as the guards on the bridge, but something told her this was the business end of the deal. The outward focused command center. This is where Tale kept his goods. The bridge was where he kept his trainees. Which meant these guards meant business. They would find out soon.

52
DAVIS

It didn't take Davis long. He knew what Ivan expected him to do with the items he'd risked his life to give him. It was a get-out-of-jail-free bundle. The makings of a Molotov cocktail. He just needed the guard to come back in the room when he was ready.

Davis chuckled to himself and had a devilish smile as he unscrewed the hilt again and pulled out the lighter within the base of the knife, "Bastard," he said. "Ivan never did like that guy." *That guy* was the guard with the beard, Robby. The one coming and going from their cell.

Davis handed one of the blankets to the kid in the next cell. "Warm up the bottle with your body heat as much as you can. Hold the bottle out like this with the cap off. Use it like a squirt bottle. Put the blanket over your arms and cover yourself. You'll most likely soak yourself too in the process. Best to avoid burns when possible. When he comes in, wait until he's closer to the cell before you spray him. Do you understand? It's important that you understand."

Jason rolled his eyes and nodded his head.

"I'll take that as a *yes*, you silent, sarcastic shit."

Davis then held the knife, blade down, in his right hand. He stood tall, rolled his head from one side to the other and shook out his arms. The next few moments had 'hairy situation' written all over them. He wanted to be ready. The kid also prepared himself.

"Stop, drop and roll. You know what that means?"

"Yeth!" Jason said.

"No...no talking from you. Only nodding or hand gestures. That's just...creepy. Be ready," Davis said, as he held the bottle against his skin, attempting to warm the liquid. Later, he moved over to the far end of his cell. Cringing at the sound of fabric tearing, Davis slowly tore a strip of his blanket off and stuffed one end into the bottle and then moved his left hand, with the bottle, through the cell bars to the other side. With his right hand he prepared to strike the lighter on the other side of the railing. Timing was everything. The guard would see the set-up as soon as he walked into the room. Davis needed to wait until he was close enough to grab. The problem was, there was no way the plastic bottle would shatter when he threw it at him. That's why he needed Jason to expel the propellant ahead of time for maximum effect.

Now, they only had to wait.

53

IVAN

He couldn't even explain it to himself. One second, he was getting the children ready for bed, which meant him yelling, "Go to bed" the moment he walked through the door; the next he found himself in the kitchen preparing the bottles. He shouldn't do this. It was a death sentence for him and the kids in the next room. He knew this. But he found himself popping the cap off the vodka bottle anyway. Searching in a cupboard for the two water bottles. Pulling the lighter out of his back pants pocket and taking the knife with the hollow hilt out of his go bag. Something in his reckless conscience told him this was really the only way he could help his friend, who'd become his brother. It wasn't his fault if Davis failed in the process. He would at least get the hell out of there.

Shrugging his shoulder as he emptied the water into a plastic pitcher, he mumbled to himself. "I'll just blame it on Robby. He's a weasel anyway." Planning to pass suspicion on to the guard, Ivan carefully poured the clear liquid into the emptied water bottles. Forever caught conning for favors of booze and goods, Robby was as incompetent as they came. He preyed on the troubled and the helpless. Ivan had no sympathy for the man. It didn't matter in the end. He could give his old friend Davis a chance to avoid an imminent death and take care of a menace at the same time. He only hoped Davis succeeded. The man had a mangled left arm and he looked like hell. If he kept this up, he wouldn't last much longer, no matter how Ivan intervened.

Holding his arm steady as he began pouring the second bottle, Ivan sloshed a little of the precious liquid over the rim when the girl walked into his peripheral view. He only caught sight of her dark brown hair at waist level. "What the hell are you doing? I said go to bed."

He immediately concealed the bottle by his side, hiding his crime.

She had the tip of her right finger in her mouth. It annoyed him when she did that, partly because he knew she needed someone to care for her more than he ever could. There was no way that was ever going to happen. She was stuck with him and he was an inadequate caregiver. The only thing he could do for her and the boy was to give them shelter and food. That was all. The boy, especially, needed more right now.

The girl before him startled back a few steps at his rebuke. She pointed to the bedrooms at the back of the house.

"What?" he yelled. "Speak. What is it? I don't have time for this," he yelled louder.

She was a little thing, barely eight years old, if that, and tiny as a wisp. He'd taken her in because he caught Robby, the menace, leering at her in the lock-up one day. She was just a little girl, but had Ivan not walked in when he did, he was sure Robby would have violated her in some way. Just another reason he hated the creeper.

"He's...wet," she said and scrunched up her nose.

Ivan lowered his head. "Shit. All right, go to bed," he said calmer. He was not a parent. Didn't want to be a parent. Not in this world. Not in the last. But here he was, in charge of two children in the last month.

The girl scampered off and Ivan turned to watch her go. She was a delicate little thing, like a fawn that lost its mother. She talked to no one but him or Linda, the doctor. Perhaps instead of the boy, he should have grabbed one of the wives in those last few seconds. She needed a woman and Linda wasn't available. There was no time to really consider the consequences then. There was never a good time for consequence considering. Those days were over. You just acted now. Acted on fear and instinct. He wasn't sure why he grabbed the older boy over the younger. He wasn't sure why he grabbed that boy over the others. He just did. Perhaps it was only because he was the nearest soul to save. The path of least resistance. That's all life really was now.

He finished filling the vodka bottle and screwed on the cap. Then, he swirled the remaining liquid in the bottle and took a deep chug and let his boots fall loose against the wood floor as he walked toward the back rooms of the dark house and the boy with the pissy pants.

54

JASON

This wasn't wise, Jason thought as he held his arms through the bars of the cell, holding an opened bottle of warm vodka that his cellmate was about to ignite as Jason sprayed the contents onto the guard with the beard. He didn't like the guy either, but he didn't want to cause anyone unnecessary pain and so far, the worst thing the bearded guy did was call Ivan the Adopter, chopper, clopper...whatever it was. He didn't think the guy deserved to go up like a Roman candle. But that was just him. Maybe Davis and Ivan knew the guy better, and Jason was beyond the idea of finding out if the guy deserved this or not for himself. He just wanted to get out of there, find a radio, and give his position. He still felt like he owed that much to Sloane and the others.

Because he couldn't hear a thing, he kept glancing at Davis to see if he would give a signal when he heard the guy coming in the room. It had been a while and the guard did seem as if he came in at certain intervals.

With the blanket layered over his arms, Jason hoped the incendiary would not backfire into the aerated stream. But hope was in short supply and like Davis said before, did he want to die in the cell or out of the cell? It was his choice and he'd made it, but was it too late to change his mind?

That's when Jason noticed the door handle begin to turn.

55

SLOANE

They hurried as they walked between the buildings with quick, even steps. Sloane could not help but pull Wren behind her with a motherly tug of her hand, which Wren flung away at first detection.

Sloane accepted this, both not being able to resist the mothering and the rejection at the same time. There were some things mothers could not do, and one was *not* to mother. Some switch somewhere gets turned on after the birth of a child and it cannot be turned off...metered, but not turned off like a light switch.

Rejection of the mothering, on the other hand, came with the maturity of the child. That, she expected—hoped for, even. Or else, she wasn't doing her job right.

"Stay out of the light," she warned them with a whisper. "Stay to building shadows as much as you can. Don't make yourself a target."

"They're not even paying attention," said Wren. "I bet we could walk right up the street."

Sloane watched the guards. Neither of them looked around too much. One of them had his rifle slung around his back, warming his hands out against the fire. The glowing dot of a cigarette hung slack from his mouth.

"Let's keep it that way. Watch your footing and no talking from this point on. Watch for trip wires and traps. Stay close."

They'd already crossed the main street, hopscotching from building to building. Soon they'd have to decide which path to take the rest of the way. Both routes held risks. Along the Riverwalk, behind the rooms of a one-story hotel, or cross the open expanse and continue jumping from building to building, making their way to the back?

Sloane put off the decision until they neared the shadows of the last building.

They held there for a minute when Chuck signaled to Boyd to keep watch behind them and then inched forward and lightly asked, "Is there a way into the back of the building? Did Marvin mention anything about that? We're not getting through the front without a battle. That's a given."

"No, he didn't. I got the impression he was hardly ever in there. He and his team were only the outside detail, for beyond their borders to the south."

"So we don't even know what floor he's on?"

"No, but Marvin did say the holding cell was in the basement of the building. That's all I know. If Jason is here, he's likely in there."

Wren butted in, "Then we need to hurry and get in there."

"Shh, you're not talking right now. I'm talking," Chuck said, pointing to himself.

Wren glared at him.

Chuck returned his attention to Sloane and said, "Then we need to..."

"Wait," Sloane whispered and pushed them back against the wall as she turned forward. A sound...a motor was coming in the distance.

They all looked and watched as the guards around the fire

turned to the north and began walking toward headlights in the distance.

"Where are they going?" Wren asked.

Chuck strained to see farther than his height. "It's the big bridge from Washington. Someone's coming."

"This is our only chance. We'll move while they're distracted. Come on," Sloane said.

56

DAVIS

The door opened in the cell room.

Davis nodded his chin. "Hey Robby," he smiled at him. *Keep coming.*

Robby stopped. Davis could see he knew something wasn't right. His arm still remained on the door. "What's..."

"I've got something to tell you, but I don't want the kid to hear. Can you...come closer?"

Robby let the door fall shut but stopped about halfway in the room. "The kid's deaf. I'm not coming any closer. What do you want?" Robby asked, his brows scrunched up.

"That's okay...that's close enough."

Davis gave the signal.

Jason pulled the opening of the bottle from his mouth and shot a stream of the vodka at the guard. He jumped back, avoiding most of the blast.

"What in the hell is going on?" Robby said.

And Jason used his right hand to swing the bottle up and down, catching the guard in the beard and all up and down the front of his shirt with the rest of the liquid, causing the guard to divert his attention away from Davis.

Davis lit the wick of his own bottle on fire.

"That better not be..." the guard said before he lit up in bright yellow flames.

He wasn't the only one.

The kid next to him in the locked cell was also was on fire around his hands and arms, despite the aid of the blanket.

"Come here, you bastard," Davis yelled at the guard as he writhed around, trying to stamp out the flames covering his chest, face and hair. The entire floor where most of the vodka had spilled was running a flaming river toward the drain in Jason's cell.

When Robbie came within reach, despite the flames, Davis reached out and grabbed him by the belt and pulled him near enough to grab the keys from his pocket.

He unlocked his cell door and shoved the flaming guard into the corner of the room and unlocked Jason's cell as he batted away the flames. Jason had retreated to the back of his cell, without room to put out his flaming clothing. Davis pulled the kid to the floor and rolled him around, slapping out the flames.

"You okay? I said stop, drop and roll. Didn't you get that part?"

He didn't give Jason the chance to respond. Instead, he pulled him up by the front of his singed shirt and dragged him from the cell.

The guard had slumped in the corner of the room, trying to put out his own flames with hands that were still ablaze. His beard seemed to be providing fuel for the fire lighting up his head. Davis almost felt sorry for him, but he didn't help the man. Instead, he grabbed the big knife and the blanket from his own cell.

The kid stood there in a daze near the door as Davis tried to decide how best to approach a man impersonating a Roman candle. He first threw the blanket over the man's head and then used the knife to cut his neck, spilling his blood down the front of him. Most of the flames were doused by then, by either the blanket or the blood.

The sickening smell of burnt hair and other body parts was not something Davis would forget. He wasn't after mercy, however. Davis wanted the man's gun and hoped it was still operational after all that.

He turned the burned body over and found the man's back holster and pulled the weapon free. "Good, let's go," Davis said, but when he turned around, the kid was nowhere in sight.

57

IVAN

He heard the alarms. They squealed in the distance, yet Ivan kept his temperate pace toward the doorway. He opened it to the cold breeze outside. It was a refreshing change to the fetid air inside the house. In his right hand he held the boy's piss-soaked blue jeans. He lifted them up and flung them in the middle of the yard. He didn't do laundry. They'd find the boy another pair somewhere. In the meantime, the girl let him wear a pair of her pajama pants that Linda had found for her. They were pink with butterflies and too big, but beggars couldn't be choosers. The boy had not yet stopped crying and Ivan wasn't sure how he felt about wearing girls' clothes. When he left the kids, the girl was rolling up the cuffs of his girly pants and covering him up with her own blanket. The girl was a nice one. She seemed happier having someone smaller to take care of. He wasn't yet sure about the boy.

In his left hand, Ivan held his pistol. He checked the magazine, out of habit more than anything else. It was fully loaded but he knew that already. It was a habit, a mere stall for time. When he was through, he stood there watching the night from the doorway while the alarms, fed by a generator, were still wailing in the direction of the building housing Davis.

Someone was going to die tonight.

"Stay inside," Ivan yelled into the dark emptiness of the house and shut the door behind him as he left.

58

JASON

He took the first and only chance he had to run. Davis had his back turned as he doused the Roman candle and though it hurt, Jason used the back of his burned arm to open the door and skirted through the opening without Davis noticing. Adrenaline pumped through his veins as he ran up the dimly lantern-lit stairs. Flames reflected off the walls in a flickering dance. Jason hit a corridor with an open door at the end of it. He looked both ways and then took off at a run toward the open doorway at the end of the long hall but ducked when he saw shrapnel flying off the side of the wall in front of him. He turned and saw Davis, with only parts of a torn and burned hospital gown clinging to his front as he stood over another body.

That guy was relentless with the killing.

Jason's eyes met his in the dim lamplight of the hallway.

With one fling of his hand, Davis waved him on, but then crouched and turned to the opposite side as if he knew someone was coming.

Jason didn't stay to find out whom; he ran through the door's exit and out into the cover of darkness with the song *You're Gonna Go Far, Kid by The Offspring* running through his mind. He had no idea where he was, but firelight came from one direction. He went in the other, farther into the darkness.

The one thing that kept coming back to him was the radio he saw in Ivan's hand the moment they were taken. If he could get to Ivan, he might find a way to alert the others.

But that would have to wait, because at the moment, he had to hide. Toward the firelight, there were silhouettes of guards and other people in the distance, running from building to building. He couldn't let anyone capture him now. He had to make the most of this opportunity and to do that, he needed to find the least likely place they would search for him.

59

SLOANE

They began to run, all of them, across the open expanse to the back of the building when suddenly Sloane saw a man dart out of the back-side door. "Down," she whispered, and they all crouched again behind a truck. "Stay down," she said as she peeked through the vehicle's windows. The man seemed familiar, but she wasn't sure.

She tapped Chuck on the shoulder and flicked her index finger twice, then pointed through the glass.

She motioned with her chin, and he looked as well at the running man.

Chuck nodded and in the lowest tone possible whispered, "That's the man we let get away."

"Are you sure?"

He nodded, but Sloane wasn't sure.

"Wren," she said with a tilt of her head.

Her daughter nudged Chuck over and looked too. "That's him! That's the guy who took Jason," she said in a loud whisper.

Sloane nodded her head.

The man ran on.

"Aren't you going to do something? He's getting away," Wren said.

Shaking her head, Sloane said, "No. He's not our objective."

Her daughter let out a frustrated breath and pulled her knife.

"No," Sloane said. "He's not why we're here. You attack him, and we *all* lose our cover."

Wren turned away but glared at her mother.

But it was too late for the man getting away anyway. Sirens suddenly erupted, causing them all to scramble for cover.

"Stop, Davis, or I'll shoot!" yelled a voice and the beam of a large flashlight lit up the man running away.

Sloane and Chuck pulled Wren down and out of sight behind the vehicle.

"We have to move," Chuck said.

"Why are they after him?" Wren said, and Sloane knew they were all wondering the same thing, but there was no time to figure that out now.

"Quick," Sloane said and led the others to the side of the next building.

Guards were suddenly running everywhere with the sound of the alarm. Something big was going on.

"Are they after *us*?" Boyd asked.

"I don't think so," Sloane said.

"Then what?" Wren said. "What the hell's going on?"

"I don't know, but as far as I can tell, Jason is still in that building and that's where we need to go."

"Drop your weapon," the guard yelled as the man named Davis stood in the middle of a parking lot. He was naked except for a small cloth barely hanging onto his chest and held a pistol in one hand and a long knife in the other.

Sloane watched as the guard with the flashlight approached closer.

"Don't do this, Davis. Put down your weapons," one of the guards said.

"Where are my wife and boys? Did he kill them? Someone tell me the goddamn truth!" Davis yelled.

Another guard ran up to the man in the flashlight and said something no one could hear.

"Davis, Tale is coming. Put down your weapons."

Davis held each weapon away from his body and shook his head. "No. You want them? Come and take them."

To the right, several others were coming. Sloane assumed this was Tale with his inner entourage. She raised her rifle and trained her scope on the center figure in the dark, but she wasn't yet sure which of them was Tale. If she could just take him out, this would all go much smoother.

"Kill him," yelled the commander's voice.

Sloane quickly switched her aim to the guard with the flashlight as he raised his rifle and pulled the trigger, before he could take down Davis.

Davis jumped back, confused, but then quickly began firing on the guards in front of him.

Sloane quickly regretted her last-minute decision as the guards began to also shoot in their direction.

"Go, go, go," she yelled as her group ran for cover. At the last second, she saw that Tale and his men had fled but Davis was still fighting like a one-man army.

Out of breath but safe, Chuck said, "Was that one of those *enemy of my enemy is my friend* maneuvers? Because I'm trying to understand why you did that."

She shook her head. "Not exactly. That was a *be the one to control the chaos* maneuver. We still need to get into that building. I don't know why they're after him or what the hell's going on but that Davis guy is pretty pissed off at Tale. Let's stay out of his way. He's causing enough of a disruption to mask our moves for now."

"Is he still standing?" Wren asked.

"I'm not going back to find out," Chuck said with crazed eyes. "That guy is nearly naked, armed and killing everyone there. Did you see him? I can't believe we let him go. We should have cloned the guy. Made a whole army out of naked black soldiers."

"That's...not right," Wren said, shaking her head.

"Shut up! Both of you," Sloane said as she tried to figure out their next move. So far, they had to retreat back to one of the previous buildings because of infighting. Shots and shouts still rang out in the distance. Ragged beams of light told her someone was running in one direction and still others in another direction.

Things quieted after a few seconds. Sloane put her hand out to indicate the others should stop their chatter. "Davis must be on the run now," she whispered.

"Or...he's dead," Wren said.

"Nah...that guy's invincible," Chuck said.

Wren and the others stifled laughs.

"We're going now, children," Sloane said with her eyes drilling into Chuck.

❧ 60 ❧

DAVIS

Davis had no idea where the shot came from that saved him, but he suspected Ivan was there in the shadows somewhere to help him. He wasn't sure what had changed his mind or if he was always on board. He knew when Ivan had taken in the girl, that changed things for him. "That's the way kids are," Davis had warned him. "They crush your heart. They'll make you do anything to ensure their safety. Watch out for that. Things you wouldn't normally consider."

At the time, Ivan denied anything would change him. He'd been wrong, of course. Davis knew that. The girl was an innocent. She'd been a prisoner of Hyde's. They were sent to pick her up and ordered to kill her. Only Davis had children of his own and he wouldn't do it. Ivan couldn't either. He was just too decent. The only alternative was to make her useful to them. To prove to Tale she had some value. Ivan knew the radios. He taught the girl and quizzed her, became her friend and over time pulled information from her about the town of Cannon Beach. This information became especially useful when Hyde and his entire operation were destroyed.

That's when Tale agreed to let Ivan adopt the girl that he kept in the lock-up all by herself. He needed a solution under Tale's terms anyway. This arrangement provided that. The thing was, though, Ivan was not father material.

Davis had laughed at the time. Nowhere in Ivan's DNA was a carved niche for sensitivity. It just wasn't in his makeup. But the girl seemed capable of taking care of herself anyway.

Though as Davis ran toward his house in some faded hope that his wife would be standing there in the doorway, his heart ached knowing his own children were no longer a part of this world. He loved being a father. He needed to see the empty house for himself. Know that they were all gone from this world. Perhaps she left a note? Then he'd find some damn pants and go after Tale for the last time. He wasn't leaving this world with that man still breathing.

The other guards were still after him. He'd killed four of them before he could get away. The funny thing was, he regretted doing the killing. He was just good at it. He knew if Tale were dead, they'd turn human again. Or so he hoped. Maybe they were too far gone now. He'd seen that happen in war, back in the old days, when things were run by the careless greed of man, until nature put a stop to that.

His feet were so messed up as he landed one in front of the other over torn asphalt, glass, and gravel, it didn't matter. He felt nothing anymore. It only mattered that he made it to the house, regrouped and returned to end this madness once and for all.

61

IVAN

Later he would wonder why he bothered. It seemed important at the time. Davis was more than wounded and probably dead, so why not get Linda? She was the doctor, right? He found himself standing in her doorway, looking at her with a smile as all hell broke loose behind him. People ran in different directions, panic-laden shouts and orders dissipating on the wind. But he smiled at her and reminded himself how beautiful she was even though she sported one hell of a black eye.

"Where's your guard?"

Her returned gaze was equally quizzical. One corner of her mouth lifted in a smirk.

"He ran off to help the others?" she said with her shoulder raised. And then with a tilt of her head, she asked, "Davis?"

He assumed she referred to all the noise in the distance. "I believe so," he said. "Get your things. He'll need your help."

She let go of the door and stood there with a sudden stubbornness. "If I leave this house, Ivan, I'm not coming back. You can't make me."

Her lips were now in a thin line. The smirk disappeared.

With a tilt of his head he said, "I have no intention of making you do anything you don't want to do. Like I said, get your things."

With a nod of her chin, she turned and ran inside. Her hair bounced like an airy cloud around her.

Ivan turned around on the porch and watched the chaos. He should be among them. They were doing it all wrong but that wasn't his job anymore. Somewhere between grabbing the boy from his dead mother and nearly betraying his friend, he'd made an important decision. He wasn't sure what that decision was, but he was acting on it. It felt good for a change.

She touched the back of his arm. He turned around and found her standing there with not one but two backpacks. Her hair was tied up under a hat. He didn't like that, but it was probably for the best where they were going.

"Where is he? Davis, I mean."

"I don't know. Let's follow one of these idiots. We're bound to catch up to him."

Then a few shots were fired nearby, and he found himself pulling Linda to the porch flooring.

"I'm betting that's him. Let's go."

62

JASON

Jason couldn't hear the shots, but he saw intermittent flashes in the distance. Someone was in big trouble. It was probably whoever was on the other end of Davis. He wasn't going anywhere near there. He still resented him for manhandling Wren and kidnapping him. Jason wasn't sure what his motives were or what was going on with the big dude, but he'd rather not run into him again.

He'd forgotten what it was like to be held against his will and tortured. His time free in Cannon Beach held more value. It was strange how the mind worked sometimes. Pain and affliction seemed like a fleeting memory once it was all over. It wasn't like a happy memory...those you kept forever. Or like the loss of a loved one...those stayed with you. He'd once heard that if mothers remembered the extensive pain of childbirth, they wouldn't do it more than once. It was only when Jason felt the stinging burns along his arms that he flashed again on the torture room, and Hyde, and the hell he endured in there.

But that was over, and this was now. Jason scanned the streets up and down. Blue truck, blue truck...that was all he could think of now. Finding the blue truck and the man who drove it. None of the other guards that he saw wore a hand-held radio but that guy. Someone had to be on the other end of that thing, but it wasn't a walkie. It was a genuine radio, with longer distance capability. He needed to find one and get word to Sloane quick, because something was going down here.

A few more streets over and Jason had to take cover behind a vehicle as guards ran by. He was about to run to the next building when he turned back suddenly. He'd spied through the window a residential house across the darkened street and in the driveway was the blue truck Ivan drove that day.

Jason stood straight up despite the chaos. *Hmm, maybe he's home.* Despite the dangers around him, Jason ran over to the truck and tried the handle. It was locked. Dammit. He looked inside the darkened cab, but the radio was either not inside, or perhaps it was inside the house with its owner?

Across the yard, Jason began to walk up to the front door as if he belonged there, thinking of the song *The Man Comes Around by Johnny Cash*. The house was like something out of the post-war era. It was in desperate need of repair but looked comfortable. There were several things flung in the yard; he couldn't really make out what they were in the dark. A few figures ran from one direction to the other across the street. They didn't seem to mind him. He wasn't who they were looking for, apparently. Davis was the person they were seeking at the time, he suspected. That could change, though; he needed to complete his mission and get out of there.

Jason put his hand on the doorknob and expected to find it locked but when he twisted it, the door opened with a creak. He stepped inside and closed the door behind him. He assumed Ivan was out helping Davis. This was probably a good place to hide for a while. He scanned the darkened living room for any radio equipment, figuring it was like a drone...you couldn't have just one. You had to have a couple of different models, right? One was never enough. But there were limited supplies for a radio head at worlds end.

The kitchen. That's where everyone put their stuff. They dumped their change, their keys, their junk mail all over kitchen counters. Nodding to himself, Jason headed to the kitchen that he figured was down a short hallway. When he rounded the corner to a short galley, Cash's music suddenly ceased. What he didn't find was any radio equipment. What he did find was a set of eyes staring back at him, and they were from someone half his size.

63

SLOANE

"I can't help it if I talk when I'm nervous," Chuck said as they ran toward the back of the port authority building.

"Just stop," Sloane said. She had no idea how she put up with the guy when suddenly, as she had her back turned, a close shot rang out. When she looked, a guy fell in the parking lot behind them.

"What?" Chuck shrugged. "He was aiming at you. I didn't have time to warn you."

She didn't say anything. She peeked inside the open doorway to find a long hallway, lit at the end by lantern light. "Marvin said he's probably in the basement. Let's look for a stairwell on this floor."

"Now I smell something burning?" Wren asked.

But no one had an answer for the smoky aroma so prevalent in the hallway.

Sloane motioned for half the team to remain in cover outside while she and the rest, including Chuck and Wren, went inside. She posted Boyd as the lookout in-between.

Sloane took the lead as they formed a line against one side of the hall and made their way through. She stopped when she saw what she was looking for. "Stairs," she said and motioned for the rest to follow her. Before she went down, she saw that Boyd was watching them from the opened doorway. He gave a thumbs-up, and she held an ironic hope that she wasn't seeing him for the last time as she and the others behind her descended the stairs. She realized he was one of them now.

At the end of the concrete stairs was an open doorway to a darkened room. There was only a little light coming through small rectangular windows at the very the very top of the wall. But she could barely see through them for the smoke that was so thick it burned their eyes.

She used a small flashlight.

"Ja-son?" gasped Wren immediately in a tone that threatened their cover.

Sloane grabbed her daughter and cast the light to the side of the room and found a body leaning up against the wall. There was no hair on his head and his face was unidentifiable. Blood and char soaked the entire front of him. What got to her the most was the man's hands and fingers were formed in a kind of claw, a sign of his agonizing death.

"Calm down, that's not him," Chuck said.

"How can you tell?" Wren asked as she held her nose and bent over, nearly retching.

Chuck knelt down and touched the dead man's boot. "Because your boyfriend wouldn't be caught dead in these. Besides, they're two sizes too big."

"Both the cells are open. He must have been in here," Wren said.

"It's possible but there's no sign of him in here now," Sloane said.

Then Boyd's frantic whisper echoed down the stairwell. "Someone's coming. Hurry!"

64

DAVIS

Davis allowed himself to stop in the silence of his home. With the door closed behind him, he stood there in total dark. The utter quiet cut him through his core and weighed like a sickness in his soul. His hands were shaking. He knew he'd been a fool to have any shred of hope they were alive.

"Oh, Cecile...I'm sorry. I'm so sorry!" he cried as he imagined his wife and boys ripped from this home. He tore through then, clear to the back of the house where the room he shared with her was, avoiding any glance at the boys' room as he went. He couldn't bear that. Not now.

Inside the master bedroom, he found the bed unmade. Something Cecile never tolerated three steps after she'd risen for the day.

In his mind, he began to piece the scenario together. They took them at night or early the next morning. "Dragged my wife and boys from their beds?" His voice quivered with anger as he could not help but picture them in front of a firing squad as he'd seen others in the past before them and did nothing about their peril.

He flung open a drawer and then another. Soon he found himself pulling a shirt on over his wounds and socks over his shredded heels. He dressed and tied the laces to his boots. He refilled spare magazines with hidden ammo and grabbed a couple of other items Tale wasn't aware he had in his possession.

Those people beyond the bridge. That boy he dragged back here against his will. They were never the enemy, only an offering for mercy. Tale was the enemy and now Davis had nothing to lose. So Tale would pay.

A gravelly voice then came out of the shadows and into the dim ambient light from the window. "What do you think you're doing there, buddy?"

65

JASON

"Uh...hi," Jason finally said after the girl before him finally darted her attention around Jason. "Where's Ivan?" she said timidly.

Jason could tell she was afraid of him.

"..eye...doughn know," Jason said slowly, trying to hit all the vowels and consonants with the part of his tongue that remained.

She backed away.

"Wai...wai. I wone hur you."

The girl looked skeptical. "You talk funny."

Jason agreed and nodded. He smiled then.

"What's your name?"

"Das-son."

"Jason...you mean Jason?"

He nodded.

"My name's Elsa," the girl said.

66

IVAN

It was him, or it had been Davis, they'd shot at. He was gone now and what remained were four dead bodies. Linda bent to check one.

"Don't...don't bother. We've got to go."

"But they might need help," Linda said, tugging on his arm.

Ivan looked around. "I don't think so, darlin'. Davis doesn't leave a job half-ass, typically. I think I know where he's headed first, though. If we catch up to him, we can all get the hell out of here."

"Why should we stop him from doing what needs to be done?"

"Because you and I both know he'll die in the end. He'll kill Tale, but he'll die, too."

She nodded, knowing that was the truth of things. "Let's go, then."

He'd always liked Linda. She was a practical woman.

They kept out of sight as they ran two more blocks and down an alleyway. Ivan could always find Davis's house in the dark. They'd both rambled the path between their homes in the pitch black of night, drunk in an attempt to mask the things they had to do for Tale.

"How do you know he's inside?" Linda whispered.

"I don't. He would have come through the front door. He'd expect me to come through the back as usual. That way we don't get shot, maimed or killed before he realizes it's us. You ought to stand back, though, just in case." Ivan made purposeful strides up the back steps as he approached the door. He banged on the door with his customary ease in hopes Davis would recognize his old familiar pattern.

The first three raps brought no response. Ivan leaned closer to the door with his good ear. He looked at Linda standing by herself in the dark. He reached for the handle. It opened with ease. Perhaps the door was always unlocked, though Ivan had never tried to open it on his own before. He stepped inside the darkened hallway, then motioned for Linda to remain outside. She slunk into the shadows of the detached garage and waited. He stepped inside and then closed the door behind himself.

"Davis?"

There was nothing. No sounds at all. The home was nothing more than an eerie crypt to a once-happy family's memory. He stood there for a while, remembering the children's chatter...the aroma in the kitchen as Cecile baked.

He had a hard time swallowing with the lump that formed in his throat. There were many homes like this in Astoria now that only carried the memory of a happy family...most of them were dead now. It had to stop.

Then with a creak coming from the front door of the house, Ivan stepped back into the shadows of the laundry room. He glanced out the back window, seeing the bare outline of Linda safe in the dark as someone came through the front door.

His pulse quickened until he recognized his old friend's familiar footsteps. As the seconds passed, Ivan decided it was best to let his friend have his moment before he revealed himself. As hard as it was to overhear Davis's pained sentiment, Ivan shook his head in the dark, wishing he could reach out and help his friend. But he knew that was impossible at the moment.

He heard him bear his weight down onto the creaking bed in the master bedroom. Heard him fling open drawers, and he knew then that his friend had crossed the bridge from regret and failure to maddening anger and revenge.

This was why he was here. Ivan knew he had to stop the man, or slow him down at least. There were things he wasn't aware of, precious things.

67

SLOANE

The three of them raced up the stairs, joined by Boyd, as several voices descended from the upper floors. As they sprinted to the light at the end of the tunnel, Sloane wished she could hear what the people who were coming were saying, get some clue as to where Jason might be.

They ran through to the outside, just in time, and Sloane's people continued on to the sanctuary of the next building as they avoided the chaos around them.

There were a few times during this whole process that Sloane knew their mission would change from a search and rescue to destroy. She wanted to find Jason first. But that didn't seem possible now.

"Maybe he escaped?" Boyd suggested.

"That wasn't him in there? Are you sure?" Wren pleaded with Chuck.

"I told you, it wasn't him," Chuck said.

"He's got to be out here somewhere then," Wren insisted.

Sloane had not said a word yet. She let their words come out first and then waited for a lull in the conversation, as well as a decline in her rapidly beating pulse.

After taking a deep breath, she looked at her daughter, knowing what her reaction would be, and then said to everyone, "Listen...this is where our mission changes. We're no longer looking for Jason. We don't have any leads. We're going back down there. The enemy has trapped themselves. There's no way out from the cell room but up. We'll take them out and then regroup. I don't think Tale was among them, but we'll take them down one by one until we find him." She stared into her daughter's eyes again and so wanted to say...*but you're staying here.* She couldn't. Wren was just a good a shot as any of them and she'd proven herself capable. Sloane had no excuses to hold her back... no excuse to protect her. Hell, she needed her in this. She needed Wren to fight just like everyone else.

"Mom, he's still alive. I can feel it," Wren said, even though a second ago she doubted the burned man wasn't Jason.

"Wren...we're not giving up on Jason. We're just switching gears," Sloane said.

"I'm not leaving without him," Wren said defiantly, with a shake of her head.

Chuck intervened before Sloane could say anything. "Take all that fucking drama, Chica, and bottle it. You're going to need it in the next few seconds. Understand?"

"We're wasting time. Let's..." Sloane began to say when her radio buzzed.

"Sloane...You there?" Kent asked. His voice was hopeful and excited.

"Yes. Are you okay? Did something happen?" Sloane said.

"Listen...he contacted us. He's escaped!"

"Thank God!" Sloane said.

"You can all head back now. He's coming this way...and he says he's bringing two little girls. Sloane...one of them is Boyd's sister. Watch out though...we keep hearing a lot of gunfire in the distance. A lot of the guards are going your way."

Air escaped Sloane's lungs then as she tried to think about

what was most important. Her first inclination was to fight Tale. Kill him and end the craziness. She heard the gunfire in the distance, too. Her eyes flickered to her daughter and then to Boyd.

"I believe that's infighting you're hearing. They're going after that guy that took Jason. He's one hell of a fighter. We're confused as to why but whatever. Jason will never get across that bridge. Did you tell him how to get to the boats?" Sloane said while Wren burst into happy, relieved tears.

"Yes, he's going there to wait for you. You have to hurry, Sloane. Get the hell out of there. I don't know what's going on but stay out of the line of fire. Marvin said the shots sound like Davis is in action. He won't stop for you, Sloane. Please get out of there. I've got to go. Someone's coming."

The call ended abruptly, and Sloane wasn't sure if she should be concerned for Kent's safety or not.

"My sister? Elsa's with Jason? Is that what he said?" Boyd said, stunned.

Sloane nodded, holding back tears. "He said so."

"We can't let Tale live, Sloane." Chuck voiced what was on her mind. She gave him a tight nod but smiled.

"We'll talk about it on the way. Let's get to the boat."

68

DAVIS

Davis had his hands tearing at the man before him before he realized who he was.

Ivan let him have those seconds. He didn't fight back.

"Tell me what I want to know!"

Not one for dramatics, Ivan said, "You already know, mate. She's dead. I'm sorry."

Davis still clenched Ivan's shirt front and leaned his head down as his stomach retched. To hear the words was like a gut punch. Someone finally said the words he fought to hear.

Davis stood again, released one hand, reached back and punched Ivan in the face.

After the recoil, Ivan didn't strike him back. He held him, as Davis began to sink to the floor.

"Come on, man," Ivan said with a slur. "We've got to go." He wiped the blood from his mouth with the back of his hand. "Linda's outside, she's waiting. We're leaving here after we pick up a few things from my house."

"I'm not leaving. You take Linda and go... Get out of here. I've got to end this."

"No, you don't."

A rapid knock came then...at the back of the door.

"They're coming," Linda said. "Let's go."

69

JASON

Every time he spoke it freaked out the older girl. The younger one was in some kind of trance. Jason had that one slung over his shoulder as he ran. Despite the burns on his hands and arms, he held onto Elsa with everything he had and ran through the fleeting darkness. The sun was threatening to come up on the distant horizon and he had to get these kids to the boats as fast as he could, before the light of day threatened their escape.

Elsa, thankfully, knew where the radios were in the house and helped convey the messages back to Kent. He only hoped he wasn't too late to keep Sloane from coming after him.

His conversation with Kent was short and jagged, but Kent had said that Sloane had already made it to this side of the bridge, and he'd call her off as soon as possible. To meet her at the purple building by the boats. That was all he had to do...make it to the boats with the children and meet up with Sloane. Those were Kent's words. Everything would be okay then. But that was not what happened.

70

KENT

"Don't shoot!"

In the moments before this announcement, Kent had heard a rustling noise behind him. He'd glanced at Marvin, whose eyes were bulging in the direction behind him, and ended his radio transmission with Sloane abruptly. Then Kent lifted his weapon and turned on his heel all at once. He admitted to himself he was a moment too late in his maneuvers; had the persons before him been unfriendly, he'd be toast, or at least sporting a couple more holes in his already ragged attire.

"Put your weapons down."

"We...don't have any weapons," said a small old man in a thin t-shirt and tightly belted blue jeans. He was so thin he reminded Kent of a wispy twelve-year-old girl.

"What do you want?"

"Food if you have it. But I'm not here for myself. I'm here to warn you. I've been watching, you see. Don't know what foolishness you folks are up to, but you won't make it long over there," he said, extending his scrawny, sinewy arm out over the bridge. "Sun's coming up. I asked myself if I should get involved late last night when you folks showed up. I said no then. It's near morning now and by the grace of God, you folks ought to get outta here. Nothing for you over there but death," the man said, ending with a crescendo.

"What'll happen when the sun comes up?" Kent asked.

"They'll change guards. They'll spot you right away. Take everything you have and your lives," he said, shaking his head at Kent like he was an idiot.

"He's right," Marvin said.

"Did you...not tell me something important, Marvin?"

Marvin chuckled. "No, Doctor Sinister...I'd think it was pretty apparent the bridge will become an issue once daylight arrives. That is, if there's anything left over once the gunfight's over."

Kent turned his attention back to the old man. "What do you do over here for food? Are there others?"

"Just me and my bride. She's...at...home," the old man said, choking on the last few words. His throat was closing up with emotion.

Kent decided not to ask about her. He suspected it was too late. Reaching into his bag, Kent found a ration bar. "Here, have this. Eat it slowly. And here are a couple cans of food too."

The old man put the cans in his loose pockets. His hands shook as he opened the wrapper on the bar. "Eat it slowly or you'll throw up. Stay out of sight. If we can, we'll leave you more by the bridge later. Just stay out of the way and keep safe. Do you understand?"

Kent watched the old man nod like a chastised little boy as he walked away back the way he came.

"Didn't anyone ever tell you not to give candy to strangers?"

"That was take candy from strangers."

Marvin chuckled. "Same difference. He's probably going to sell his cans for drugs."

"I'm afraid we're beyond the luxury of drug addictions now, sadly. Full-on starvation."

"Frankly, I'm surprised he's still here."

"What do you mean?"

"That old man and his wife have always lived here. We had to run off everyone else. Took everything they had. He just keeps hanging on."

Kent's stomach rolled. He shook his head and was about to say something when the gunfire across the bridge began again.

Marvin caught the look before the renewed worry. "Don't concern yourself with our souls, Doc." He shook his sweaty, pained face. "We didn't like the job. We just did what we had to do. We let them go every chance we got. Warned them to leave. Some of them were smart enough. Some stayed out of sight and some wouldn't listen. They paid with their lives, but you know...so did we."

Kent cut his eyes at Marvin. He wanted to say, *Like that makes a difference?* But he remembered Marvin's family and what he said earlier. How he knew they were likely dead already because of Tale's rules. And...to top it off, here he was lying in misery, unable to walk. In the end, Kent had no rebuff. This life they now lived wasn't fair. Instead he turned his attention to the horizon, where the light of the sun would soon come up, casting its rays against the reality of the day as it unfolded with no regard to suffering.

71

SLOANE

Sloane found it difficult to keep up with the change in tactics from one second to the next. It was like an emotional roller coaster, only with bullets whizzing past.

Instead of heading back the way they came, they had to run like hell out in the open, down the main street, hopscotching from building to building again.

"What the hell's going on? Did you hear that?" Chuck yelled.

"My ears are still ringing. What?" Sloane said back. And they were. Everyone was crouched down on the ground by then, huddled in a mass behind a cinder block building.

"That was a grenade. I'm pretty sure," Sloane said.

Chuck nodded. "We've gotta keep moving. Come on."

Her thoughts were now on Jason and the children he apparently recovered. He would not likely move very fast with them in tow.

The evergreen forest hedge was just beyond the street by then. Behind them came a Humvee, windows open, men with guns hanging out and charging fast in the direction they wanted to be. Sloane put her arm out, nearly clotheslining Boyd as she did, stopping everyone from exposing them.

"That's Tale's men," Boyd said.

"Is he in there?"

Boyd shook his head. "I don't know. I doubt it. Seems like he has others do his bidding for him. He's good at that."

"We have to get out of here," Wren said.

"We are...without dying in the process. Let's keep moving," Sloane said, knowing that dying was a real possibility. Whoever that guy Davis was, he was causing a lot of problems.

Crossing the empty expanse, they continued to hear gunfire in the distance. It came closer at times and then receded.

"There's got to be more than one person they're after, or they're really bad at this," Chuck said.

"It does sound like there's more than one battle going on," Sloane said.

Finally, they edged nearer the evergreen barrier they'd skirted through before. Only this time, they weren't the only ones taking cover shelter in the trees.

72

DAVIS

Outside, Davis heard gunfire erupt nearby. It reminded him of another time. He wasn't sure who the hell they were firing at. Then it came to him. "The kid... Shit!" Davis said and took off at a run in the direction of the firefight.

"Wait! We have to get out of here," Linda pleaded.

"You guys go without me. I got that kid into this. I owe him that."

They yelled after him, but Davis paid no attention. He ran on, with his backpack and rifle in his hands, into the mayhem.

When he rounded the final corner, most of the guards had their backs to him. They were focused on an old coffee shop building, not much more than a shed now. There were too many of them. If Jason was in there, he didn't stand a chance. Davis watched them for a second as he prepared one of the ordinances he had in his pack. He knew this was a risky move because all of their attention would refocus on him after this...that is, if he didn't get them all in one fell swoop.

He saw one of the nearby soldiers raise his weapon and Davis drew the line of sight and saw movement in the building. Before the guard could fire, Davis lit the fuse and threw the ordinance in the center of the group of guards.

The explosion knocked him down backward. With a piercing ring in his hears, Davis sat up, weapon in hand, and shook his head. He could barely see in the dark smoke. But what he did see was one guard get up and aim at Jason through the haze. He had someone with him, a child perhaps, and he ran on.

Davis shot the guard aiming at Jason and the other two that attempted to move. The rest lay still as stone.

That was when, in the distance, he saw headlights. Davis knew what that meant. The Humvees were coming. Hell, he'd trained these guys and so far, they sucked without their leader. With Jason free and clear of the trap he was in, Davis set up a trap of his own for the Humvee. If he could take the vehicle, he could get to Tale before he fled across the big bridge. More than anything, Davis wanted to kill the man and anyone who stood in his way.

73
IVAN

"What do we do? He's going to get himself killed."

Ivan looked at her and shook his head. "Nothing we can do. He's made up his mind. Come on, we have to get back to my place and get the kids."

As soon as he saw the front door of his house, he knew something was wrong. "I told them to stay inside," Ivan growled as he ran across the front lawn. Inside, the place was dark and dreary, not unlike Davis's place. He ran through the house and searched each room. Nothing.

"Girl...where are you?" he shouted.

"Where could they have gone? Do they leave the house often?" Linda asked.

"No, never."

"Oh no. Maybe it was the gunfire. They're probably scared to death. Think, where would they go?"

He threw his hands up in the air. "Hell if I know, Linda. I'm not their parents. They were supposed to stay here. Damn kids."

"It's not their fault. Christ, it sounds like a war zone out here. You can't blame them for being scared."

"Now what?" Ivan yelled. "We can't leave without them. The girl..."

"Elsa, you mean."

"Yeah, she'd only go to you or me. That's it."

"Maybe she went back the infirmary. Damn...that's where we hear most of the shooting now. Oh, Ivan."

"Stay here...I'll go look for them."

"No. I'm coming with you."

He stopped in his tracks. "I'll come back for you. I can't let you get hurt. Listen, just get out of here. Go across the bridge and wait for me. I'll grab the kids and be there as soon as possible."

She shook her head. The tight curls threatened to spring out from underneath her hat.

"I know you heard me the first time. No arguments. Go, Linda."

She didn't move at first.

"If something happens to me, I'll tell them where to find you. Someone's got to take care of them. It sure as hell won't help them if you're dead too. Wait for us there."

"You sure know how to convince a girl." She turned toward the bridge and began walking. Then she turned back and said as a warning, "Don't take long."

74

JASON

They didn't get very far before the guards spotted them. At first, Jason hoped they wouldn't fire on him as he held the two children down. There was no music to turn to now. Though he couldn't yell, in his chest he maintained a low, repetitive growl for all he was worth, as if that was going to help anything.

Apparently, firing on children wasn't a problem for these guys. They didn't seem to care. Jason and the girls made it clear to a little coffee shop stand that had seen better days.

Jason saw the evergreens ahead that Kent told him about. He said to keep heading southeast through a neighborhood. Follow the evergreen belt. It was right there, just a few streets away, but he was stuck in a shack of a building, crouched down with two scared little girls clinging to him as men shot at them, debris flinging from the blown-out glass and chunks of splintered wood showering down upon them.

We're going to die. I'm going to die here finally, but these little girls, they don't deserve this.

That's what prompted Jason to partially stand. He waved his hand through the window and searched for a place to run. If he left the girls where they were, he could draw the gunfire away from them. That was the only way to save them. He settled them low in the corner behind the concrete foundation. It wasn't much cover but that was all there was. He would have run away then, but the girls clung to him. Their little hands wrapped tightly around his arms. He couldn't tell them, "Let go, stay where you are;" they wouldn't understand. He had to break free and make a run for it, far enough to keep them out of the line of fire.

Just as he broke Elsa's grip from his own and was about to do the same with the younger girl, suddenly the ground shook beneath his feet with an explosion, sending him toppling over the girls instead.

Two things happened very quickly then. Jason got to his feet after he realized all the soldiers were down. He had a fleeting chance at saving the children and he had to take it now. There was no time to think. He pulled the younger one into his arms and grabbed Elsa's hand, and through the cover of smoke he ran for the tree line in hopes none of the soldiers survived long enough to shoot at them again, as the tune *I Just Wanna Run by The Downtown Fiction* played in his mind.

75

SLOANE

What is it about a forest, even a small one, that draws humans into them in a time of crisis? Sloane wondered. After the death of her first husband, she often sought sanctuary there, hiking with her daughters then. It was where people hid things like fears, remorse, and the occasional body. The ones left out in the open were found too easily.

Here too, even with sporadic gunfire now, she saw faces of those who attempted to stay out of the line of fire. A woman and her young daughter, leaning into her lap, huddled behind a large pine. Sloane pointed her gun at the woman, warning her to stay back. The woman only stared, singing some unknown melodic tune while braiding her daughter's dark brown hair down the center of her back. The pale glimmer of the child's neck reminded her of Mae's...back home. Safe.

Sloane waited for the rest of her crew to pass her while she held her aim at the mother. Then when they were safely beyond her, Sloane tilted her head in their direction. "Come with us."

The mother never stopped singing. She shook her head and then turned her eyes back down to her daughter's braid.

Sloane couldn't understand the mother's reasoning but realized they'd all learned to cope in different ways through the madness. She couldn't save those not willing to be saved. In fact, she wasn't sure she was going to be able to fit everyone in the boats as it was, with three more additions.

When she caught up to them, they were holed up, watching something ahead. "What? What do you see?" Sloane asked.

Chuck answered, "There a group around the old man's body up ahead. The one we killed this morning...last night, I mean. Hell, whatever. I don't even know what time it is."

The light between the trees told Sloane it was early morning. And if the soldiers were on the bridge, they were going to be sitting ducks. They needed to move fast, if they wanted to get across without detection in the bright light of day.

"What are they doing? Have they discovered the boats?"

"No, the boats are still there. They're carrying the body away. We suck. We murdered that guy."

Wren looked back at them then, her eyes large pools. "I murdered that guy. And for what? We haven't even found Jason."

Just then Boyd put his hand up, shushing their conversation.

Sloane could not get forward to see what was happening. It was driving her crazy. As it was, she was stuck behind all of the others, even Chuck.

"What's..." she began to say but then something touched her in the small of her back, where no one should have been.

She turned abruptly with a swing of her rifle, thinking the mother had changed her mind. But there stood Jason, staring at her with a smile as he held onto two little girls.

Sloane lowered her rifle immediately and stifled a cry, which caused Chuck to turn around.

"Well, I'll be dammed," Chuck whispered.

Then, as Sloane watched, Jason fixed his eyes on the back of Wren's head. Her daughter was still watching the removal of the murdered man.

Jason handed off the smaller girl to Sloane and she watched him as the rest of the group parted for Jason to reach Wren.

He put his hand on the back of her shoulder. She turned around abruptly and burst into tears. Jason held Wren in his arms, comforting her.

Sloane watched this young man kiss her daughter on the top of her head.

"The coast is clear," Boyd whispered back without knowing what was going on behind him.

Sloane held Elsa's arm up as if to say, 'Look what I found.' The small crowd parted as Elsa recognized her brother, Boyd, and ran to him.

Boyd caught Elsa in his arms, nearly dropping his weapons, his eyes swimming in tears.

Chuck cleared his throat and then said, "All right, all right. Knock it off. We're not out of here yet. Everyone grim up. We've still got a long way to go."

Sloane still held the other little girl in her arms. There didn't seem to be anyone for this lost child. It wouldn't be the first time Sloane took in an orphan. She certainly wasn't going to leave the child on her own. Though they'd achieved what they were after, there was still a part of the plan unsatisfied. She looked at this group, unbelievably happy, and yet the work was still unfinished. She had to get them safely back home.

"Is it clear?" she asked Chuck as she kept looking behind them.

"Yeah, let's go," he said.

The little girl in her arms reached out for a familiar person... she reached for Jason. He broke away from Wren for a second and held the girl. Then they made their way to the hidden boats.

"We're still stopping at the bridge?" Chuck asked.

She nodded. "You are."

The waves were choppy.

"We're still not done," Chuck said.

"I know. I'll finish the job," Sloane said.

Chuck began to protest.

She shook her head. "Not leaving this undone. Not a chance."

She looked beyond Chuck as Jason handed the little girl to Wren, already sitting in the boat. Jason looked at Sloane then.

He nodded. He understood. He pushed the boat into the water as Boyd rowed them away. Wren's face was horrified as she stared back at them, but she didn't dare call out. Not now. She knew the risks.

Chuck left with the last boat. He still had work to do as well.

Sloane and Jason watched them sail out across the water.

"Kent," Sloane said on the radio. "The boats are coming your way. They should be there soon."

She heard the radio click then. She knew the pause meant he was processing her words.

"They?" he finally said.

Though they never really bothered with regular radio lingo, Sloane said, "Yes. I still have a few things to do. I have Jason with me. Leave, get the rest out of here. Go home. We'll catch up. Out."

76

DAVIS

Twice, he dropped his gun. Either he'd lost too much blood or the adrenaline pumping through the highway of his veins was too much too soon. Hell, he couldn't remember the last time he'd eaten. It was no wonder, but those thoughts were nothing more than fleeting concerns at the present moment. He had to get the Humvee away from those idiots and to do that, he had to think ahead.

The headlights were coming fast. He knew where they were going. The bridge south. They knew he and the others would likely flee that way. That's where Jason likely went, back the way they'd come. He had to stop the guards from making that impossible for anyone trying to flee from certain death.

He knelt, aimed and fired. It was a long shot. Those Humvees were built like tanks. He knew this but tried anyway. They'd spotted him and were now headed right for him.

That was when a blue pickup truck swerved in from the side.

"Get in," Ivan yelled.

Davis jumped into the back of the bed and fired on the Humvee as it chased them to the bridge.

Just in front of the entrance, Ivan spun to the side, blocking the Humvee's path.

Somewhere in his mind, he knew something wasn't right. Davis and Ivan continuously fired at the vehicle barreling toward them, shooting out tires, breaking glass, mirrors...anything, but the damn thing kept coming. Then it suddenly stopped. And then it hit him.

They weren't blocking the guards from the bridge.

The guards were trapping him and Ivan in.

"Ivan, get out. Run!"

It was Linda's shrill voice behind them, toward the guard station in the middle of the bridge, that got their attention.

A man held her there by the back of her wild hair, her hat nowhere in sight, a gun pointed at her temple. The man was none other than Tale himself, flanked by his inner circle.

"What we have here..." Tale said, dragging Linda before him and then using his bodyweight to fling her by the hair forward again, "...is an opportunity."

77
KENT

Inside the truck, Kent began packing things away for the drive home. Periodically he'd look through the scope of his gun out over the darkened waters, in hopes of spotting the boats in the fleeting dark as they arrived.

"You're not really going to leave here without her, are you?" Marvin said.

Kent kept his back to the man, not willing to discuss the argument going on inside his own head.

"She has no way of returning without the boats. She'll have to walk the long way around—assuming, of course, she manages to avoid Tale and his men. She won't make it, mate. And she damn sure won't succeed in her mission." He chuckled lightly. It was the drugs, Kent knew, that made him that way.

"Shut up," Kent said and that's when he turned and saw a woman running through the bridge. He grabbed his rifle and watched her through the scope. At first, he thought of Sloane, but this woman's build was different. She was nearly halfway when her hat flew off her head and over the bridge. She stopped but not because of the renegade hat. No, first one man and then two stepped out of the guard station in the center of the bridge.

"What is it?" Marvin asked.

"Wha...wait, where the hell did they come from?" Kent said.

The woman backed away. A third man stepped out of the guard station and then the first two ran after the woman as she turned and fled back the way she'd come. But she was no match for them. They caught up to her, threw her to the ground and hauled her back to the third man.

"Oh shit."

"What's going on? You can't keep doing that. The suspense is killing me," Marvin said, laughing.

Kent turned to him. "Can you sit up a little higher?"

"Well, yeah," Marvin said, and Kent helped him, then showed him what was going on through the gun's scope.

"Is this a problem for us? Is that woman in danger?"

It didn't take him long to say, "Yes, and yes."

"What do you mean?"

"That's Tale talking. The other two goons are his inner circle." Marvin paused then and said, "Shit...that's Linda. Anyone else might have a chance but he hates her. No chance in hell. Davis must be doing one hell of a job over there. She's always been confined to her house."

"Who's Linda?"

"She's the doctor."

Kent watched through the window and saw a blue truck coming fast toward the bridge and shortly after, a Humvee.

"Who's that?"

"Oh my God!" Marvin said as the blue truck blocked the entrance to the bridge. "That...would be Ivan...and apparently, Davis."

By then, Tale and his three men, as well as Linda, had retreated into the guard shack.

Puffs of smoke and tiny bursts of fire lit from the weapons being fired at the other end. The bangs came a second late to Kent's ears as they watched the scene unfold.

As if it just dawned on him, Marvin said, "Where are the boats?"

"Give me that," Kent said, reaching for the rifle and moving into position to look at the other side of the bridge, and that was when he saw the tail end of the last boat floating underneath the center of the bridge, right below the guard station. "Dammit."

When he looked back at Marvin, his eyes were wide. "You realize I have the detonator?"

Marvin said, "What a conundrum." His face was sympathetic but his sentiment still bore a shred of mirth. "Here you have the perfect opportunity to rid yourself of the menace and yet your people are trapped underneath the bridge you wish to blow up."

"I didn't need you to spell it out."

"I should have just said 'bummer, man?'"

Kent nodded. Then his attention was again drawn toward the bridge as he watched Tale pull the woman from the guard shack. The firing ceased, and they were now yelling across the bridge.

"She's a hostage?" Kent asked.

"Oh sure…hell, everyone wants Linda. She just won't have anyone. That's always been her problem."

Kent fleetingly noted Marvin's sing-song voice indicated the pain drugs were wearing thin.

"He'll kill her, without a doubt."

"Shit…what the hell do I do?" Kent said.

"Another conundrum…if you fire from this direction, they'll focus gunfire on us…killing me, of course…which ends my final problem in life, but you'll die too. Then your people will likely be discovered still trapped beneath the bridge."

Without taking his eye off the situation through the scope, Kent said, "This is a personality flaw that should have gotten you killed long ago."

"Hah!" Marvin said. "I'm just pointing out the facts, my friend. I'd say she has about thirty seconds left. What's it going to be? Save one, endanger all or let her die, the majority lives?"

229

78

SLOANE

It was the vehicle noise, the sounds of engines revving, tires squealing, and then the abundance of gunfire that caught Sloane's attention at first. One minute the boats were headed to the bridge's center safely and then all hell broke loose on the hot end. She heard the shouting and alerted Jason. They watched the drama unfold and then saw Chuck get out of his boat to set the bomb. Then as Boyd, in the lead boat, went to leave, he quickly backed up, seeing the problem above. They were trapped now, beneath the bridge with a bomb set to go off at Kent's command.

Jason tapped her on the arm.

Let's go, he meant.

They had to draw the commotion away from the bridge. If they could stop the guards in the Humvee, the hostages and the boats beneath would have a chance to escape.

79

DAVIS

One minute, Davis and Ivan were horrified to see Linda in the hands of Tale. The next, the guards in the Humvee were out of the vehicle and shooting at their feet.

"That's right, boys," Tale caterwauled to them. "Come and get her."

At one point, Davis turned quickly and aimed at one of the guards.

"Don't!" Ivan yelled and jerked Davis by the arm, back around to see that Tale had Linda standing to the side of him, his arm at full length, the pistol to her head.

She was shaking, or Davis imagined so, arms clasped tightly to her sides.

"Don't. Please let her go. We'll do what you ask, Tale. Put the gun down," Ivan shouted.

"Put down your weapons for starters," Tale said.

Davis shook his head in frustration and then tossed his gun off the side of the bridge.

"You too, Ivan. I expected more of you, my old friend," Tale said, and Davis noticed that Ivan visibly shook.

"Kind of makes me want to take a shower," Ivan said under his breath.

"Ivan, when we get closer, just make a run for her and dive over the bridge," Davis said.

"I'm not leaving you, jackass," Ivan said with a drawl.

Davis was about to argue with him, but it was then they heard gunfire from behind them, and the shots weren't aimed at them.

When Davis turned around, he saw the familiar blond hair belonging to Jason at a distance, taking cover behind the corner of a brick building. He and a woman were firing on the guards, already taking down two of them.

Without another thought, Davis turned around to see Ivan already had the same idea. He was running like hell for Linda.

That was when one of the guards dropped near Tale, only Ivan didn't have a gun on him.

Where did that come from? Davis thought but saw another man on the other end of the bridge firing on Tale and his men.

The other guard raised his gun in the man's direction and Davis began to run as fast as he could, but it was too late. The man at the other end of the bridge fell to the ground.

80

KENT

Kent grabbed the handheld radio and his rifle and ran the short distance to the bridge.

Their attention was turned to the other end. There was some kind of commotion going on. Then gunfire. Everyone had their backs toward Kent and he noticed Tale had lowered his weapon from his hostage's head. It was the perfect opportunity to kill the man, one he'd not likely get again. Kent raised his rifle, aimed and fired...and missed. Instead he hit the guard's leg next to him, causing Tale to turn in his direction, and before he could get another round off, he felt before he heard the shot that tore through his side, flinging him to the ground.

81

SLOANE

Sloane saw it happen in her peripheral view, as surreal a moment as anything ever in her life. A man was exposed at the end of the bridge. He was there one minute, while she was both receiving gunfire and shooting back. The next second, the figure in the distance was gone. In the back of her mind, she knew it was Kent, but at the time, she had no choice but to continue to distract the guards away from the boats as they fled from under the bridge.

There were many more of them, and she and Jason held them off until they heard the click of an empty magazine. Jason looked at her and shook his head. That was all they could do, and she hoped it was enough for the boats to make it to shore.

She searched the waters below, but Jason grabbed her arm and tried to pull her away. "Wait," she said and watched as a man lunged into the hostage and sent both of them off the bridge and into the water below.

"Da-vi," Jason said in alarm as the other man ran straight for Tale and his men.

82

DAVIS

He didn't know how he'd avoided the gunfire. He watched as Ivan swooped into Linda and the next thing he knew, the two of them disappeared over the railing. They were gone, just like that. It wasn't a long fall off the Young's Bay Bridge. Try something like that on the Astoria-Megler bridge and you were done for.

Once that happened...there was nothing in between him and his quest to kill Tale once and for all. He ran full on, eating the ground, except that merely thirty feet away, he felt his leg go out from under him. His left knee was blown out.

Sprawled to the ground, Davis yelled in agony.

"You thought you had me? Didn't you?" Tale yelled as he sauntered toward him, gun aimed. He laughed then, that squirrelly-ass laugh.

At least it's over, Davis thought. *At least Ivan and Linda made it. I'm done now.* It was a cop-out, he knew, but at least his own pain was over.

With his head on the cold pavement, Davis focused beyond Tale and his men. The wind blew at his sleeve. Even Tale's hair reached for the sky with the breeze as he came nearer. It was quiet for the first time in a *long* time. No gunfire. Nothing... except for a man dragging himself, with the aid of a big stick, toward the dead man at the other end of the bridge. He stooped and picked up something from the ground near the body.

Tale talked but Davis wasn't paying attention to anything that guy had to say.

The struggling man leaned on his crutch and waved both arms like an idiot and then Davis knew...he knew who the man was.

He made another hand gesture...one where both of his hands cupped into one big circle, each fingertip touching its opposite, and then he quickly released them. There was no time to think.

Marvin put his fingers in his mouth and let out a high, piercing whistle.

Tale and the others turned in his direction.

A muffled roar.

In slow motion, Davis sprang up on his good leg and yelled as he leapt over the side of the bridge, but not before the bright, flashing rumble.

83

SLOANE

The light of that morning allowed Sloane and Jason to become spectators to the end of Tale and his men. There was nothing they could do as the bridge came down. Chunks of concrete and metal blew all over. They hid for a while as the survivors of Astoria sorted things out.

When they thought it was safe, they stole a boat and rowed to the other side of Young's Bay. Back the way they'd come.

The others from the boats were surrounding two bodies on the ground. Their legs were all she could see.

"Jason!" Wren yelled and ran into his arms when she noticed them approaching.

Sloane stopped and stared, stunned. She had to see Kent for herself. She began walking again.

"No, Mom, don't," Wren said, catching her arm.

"I have to see him for myself. I have to say goodbye," Sloane said.

"Mom, you don't understand."

"Wren, let me go."

"He's not dead! She's working on him. He's lost a lot of blood."

Those sweet words sent Sloane to her knees.

Wren and Jason helped her up and together they walked near the others. They parted for Sloane to see the woman from the bridge sitting on the ground near Kent.

"Someone make a stretcher. We need to get him into the van," Linda ordered. Chuck and several others scrambled.

His eyes were closed, and he had a gash on his head that the woman was putting pressure on. But that's not what took her focus; the large red plume of blood on the rags near his side did.

"Is he yours?" The woman was speaking to her.

"Yes."

She smiled. "Good. He's going to make it."

"Sloane?" Kent murmured.

"Come here, honey. He wants you."

Sloane edged between the two bodies on the ground and crouched down, holding Kent's hand.

"You made it," Kent said and opened his eyes a slit.

Tears drained down Sloane's face. "I did," she said. "*We* did," she added.

"Only...because of him," he said, nudging his hand toward the other one, unmoving, beside her.

"Is he okay?" Sloane asked but it was the woman that shook her head quickly, *no*. It was then that someone laid a cloth over Marvin's head.

"It's okay...he wanted to go...he just did it with a bang," Kent said.

Sloane stepped away as they put Kent on the stretcher and took him away. She followed them as a gravelly voice caught up to her and asked, "Pardon me, but did you guys see the man that jumped off the bridge in the end? Did he make it?"

"You mean Davis? The guy they were fighting? No...we didn't see him after the explosion. I'm sorry."

The man she would later call Ivan smiled sadly and nodded. That's when Sloane realized he was carrying a child. She looked up and saw that it was the little girl she had taken care of earlier.

"Is she yours?" she asked.

Ivan shook his head and seemed a bit confused at first. "Uh, he's actually a boy. And, no, he wasn't mine, but he is now, I suppose."

The boy with the dark almond skin clung to him.

84

DAVIS

Six months later.

It was just like he remembered. A monstrosity. Like something out of Jurassic Park. Yet this time the gate was locked, unlike before. He banged on the metal with his fist. It felt awkward. *I mean, what else do you do to a fence like that?* he thought. He knew it wouldn't be long, knowing they'd seen him coming from miles away. He'd heard the drones stalking him as he approached.

It was Jason that opened the door. He smiled.

Davis said, "You gonna let me in?" Then he quickly started shaking his head, with his eyes held wide. "Only no fucking music this time."

Jason smiled wider and opened the door.

Sloane greeted him. "We're so happy to see you," she said. "Thank you for coming. We've heard what you've been working on in the last few months. We're grateful."

Davis nodded and felt suddenly embarrassed. "I ah, I had to do something. It took some time to heal as well."

"We all had injuries to heal from."

An awkward silence ensued.

"How's uh, your husband?"

"Kent...he's fine. He's still recovering as well. He's getting around better now. Thankfully Linda was there to take care of him. Kent's our only doctor. Having Ivan and Linda here to help us recover has been incredible."

"Oh, he's a doctor, too? I um, didn't know that." Davis couldn't seem to string more than a few sentences together at once. He felt cagey. It was hard to get back into the swing of things like normal conversations after keeping to himself for so long.

They'd just passed the spot where he'd last seen Jerry and the puddle his blood had created.

Sloane touched the back of his arm and made him jump. "Oh, sorry...why don't you come this way? Ivan is here, and he has something to show you."

Davis looked down the road at the small building Sloane had pointed to. They walked there in silence. Why didn't Ivan come to the door? He was the one that sent word over and over for him to come here. It was a question that bothered him. When he walked in, Sloane held the door open.

"Hello? He's here," Sloane said, and Davis thought she seemed too happy. What was there to be so damn happy about? The main room he walked into was empty. There was an open door straight to the back, where he heard the laughter of children and the squeaking cadence of a swing set in full motion.

"Oh...they're in the backyard. Go ahead," Sloane said, urging him forward down the narrow hallway.

"Not too high," came the words of a familiar gravelly voice. Davis could pick the man out of a crowd blindfolded just from hearing him.

"Please."

That voice! That voice stopped him in his tracks. Both his hands braced the walls on either side of him. His breath rapidly increased.

On the small of his back he felt Sloane's hand again. Her gentle voice said, "Yes. It's him."

85

SLOANE

She had to see it for herself. Though when she did, she couldn't believe how massive it was. They wouldn't stay long. Nearly winter and they still had a lot of work to do, but this was important. As it was, the wind whipped at them, tearing at their clothes and threatening to send them over the side into the wild waves below. No one said a word for fear of losing their breath. Gulls struggled on violent currents as Sloane stood there, her hair whipping across her face. The gate was a cold reminder of where they were and how far they'd come.

When they talked about the conflict, they now called it the Battle of Astoria. It was sort of the battle *for* Astoria because it was the gateway to the north. That gateway had to end until humanity settled down. It was for the protection of all the small communities trying to pull together to survive.

The Young's Bay Bridge was utterly demolished, which presented the old man near the entrance with an opportunity. He was now a ferry boat captain. Kent had set that up over time. It turned out that he and his wife were very enterprising and several pounds healthier.

They now accepted food and supplies in exchange for passage

on their ferry boat during good weather. Sloane and the others were a bit nervous on their first trip across, seeing where many of them nearly died. A place holds memories for a time and none of them were quite ready to face them; their voices and torment still reached for them from the past.

But now Sloane stood, over a year later, at the foot of a new gate, this one similar to the one at home protecting her community, only much larger, barring the entrance to their side of the Columbia River on the Astoria-Megler Bridge. No one was going to get through there. Not for generations and it would take that long, Sloane suspected, for the world to straighten out. In the meantime, they would learn to live again.

AFTERWORD

Before you go!

Sign up for A. R. Shaw's spam-free newsletter for special offers and her latest new releases here AuthorARShaw.com

Please write a review on Amazon.com; even a quick word about your experience can be helpful to prospective readers. Click or go to Amazon to write a review.

The author welcomes any comments, feedback, or questions at Annette@AuthorARShaw.com.

ACKNOWLEDGMENTS

The third book in the Dawn of Deception series, Unbeaten, was a cathartic write. Without intention, I see how some of my writing mirrors what's going on in my personal life.

No work of fiction completes itself without several helpful hands...besides the author's.

For this novel I'd like to thank my editor, Dr. Vonda for her clear and concise editing, Cheryl Deariso and Dena Virago my proofreaders, and my trusty BETA reader Michael Havelka.

Personally, I'd like to thank my son Adam for his inspiration for Jason's Northwest music taste, and my cat Henry (we rescued each other).

Each song is linked, if you read this electronically, to the source on Amazon where you may purchase to listen. If you're on an audio or paperback, please reference the songs to a retailer near you.

Also, many thanks to Sun Tzu, and *The Art of War*. Though I was searching for something else entirely, you inspired strength where I thought I had none.

ABOUT THE AUTHOR

A. R. Shaw is the bestselling author of the Graham's Resolution and Surrender the Sun series. She served in the United States Air Force Reserves as a Communications Radio Operator and then attended college as a mother of four. She's always written in what little off time she could manage but didn't start publishing her works until 2013.

Now when she isn't writing or spending time with family she enjoys, running, biking and traveling. She conquered the Spartan Sprint Race recently and lives in Ohio with her loyal tabby cat, Henry, and a house full of books.

ALSO BY A. R. SHAW

The Graham's Resolution
The China Pandemic
The Cascade Preppers
The Last Infidels
The Malefic Nation
The Bitter Earth
Graham's Resolution Boxset, Books 1-4

Surrender the Sun
Bishop's Honor
Sanctuary
Point of No Return
Surrender the Sun Boxset, Books 1-3

Dawn of Deception
Unbound
Undone
Unbeaten

The French Wardrobe

CPSIA information can be obtained
at www.ICGtesting.com
Printed in the USA
BVHW031602240420
578248BV00001B/157